RULE #4 YOU CAN'T MISINTERPRET A MISTLETOE KISS

RULE OF LOVE

ANNE-MARIE MEYER

Copyright © 2018 by Anne-Marie Meyer

All rights reserved.

No part of this book may be reproduced in any form or by any electronic or mechanical means, including information storage and retrieval systems, without written permission from the author, except for the use of brief quotations in a book review.

To my five children
I can't wait to spend every Christmas holiday with you

GRAB A FREE NOVELLA BY ANNE-MARIE MEYER

Sign up for Anne-Marie Meyer's newsletter and grab your free copy of **Love Under Contract** a Swan Princess inspired novella.

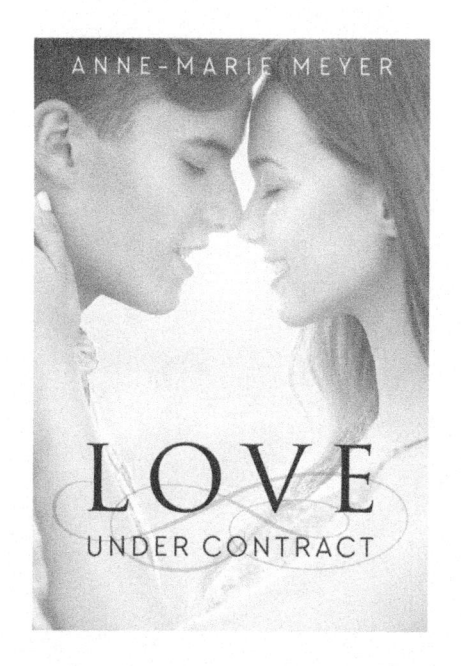

TAKE ME TO MY FREE NOVELLA

CHAPTER ONE

I stood in front of my bed, staring at the clothes I'd pulled from my closet. "Rudolph, the Red-Nosed Reindeer," played from my phone, which I'd propped up on my dresser. I hummed with the tune as I started folding my shirts.

"Hey, Ava. How's it going in here?" Mom poked her head through my open doorway.

I turned and shot her a smile. "Great. Just packing up."

Mom glanced down at her watch and then back up to me. "Good. We need to leave in twenty minutes. It's a four-hour drive to the cabin, and we want to beat the Stephensons there." A determined expression passed over Mom's face. "If we are going to win that vacation, we need to start this competition on the right foot."

I rolled my eyes. The local radio station in Little Foot, Colorado, had decided to run a Christmas contest. Show them your best Christmas spirit, and you could win a trip to the Bahamas.

Mom and Dad decided to take that challenge a step further and include the Stephensons, their best friends/rivals. At least, I think they're best friends. Some get-togethers I couldn't really tell. Everything was a competition when our families were together.

Thanksgiving football? We had to win.

The annual Easter egg hunt? We had to find the most eggs.

It was truly ridiculous how much Mom and Dad cared about beating the family they claimed were their bosom buddies.

It was one of the things I hated most about going on vacation.

"Okay, Mom," I said, moving my arms in slow motion, knowing it would send her anxiety into overdrive.

"Ava," Mom said with a warning tone.

I sighed, noting the glare she was shooting in my direction. I know she's my mom and is supposed to love me, but I may have been the reason they'd lost a few of their competitions. I was on the *don't ruin anything* train right now. I was literally just along for the ride.

Not wanting to be completely useless to my family, I gave her a smile and said, "Don't worry, Mom. I've got this." I picked up my pace as I folded and shoved my jeans into my suitcase.

She nodded towards me and the sound of roughhousing could be heard from my ten-year-old twin brothers' room. Even though trying to control my brothers was like trying to trap wind in a jar, I think my parents preferred them over me. They excelled in speed and agility. Both of which I sucked at.

Mom's forehead furrowed, and she disappeared for a moment —followed by some yelling—before she popped her head back into my room. "Hey, forgot to tell you, but Jacob is back. He'll be at the cabin." She sucked in her breath as she studied me. "I hope you're still okay joining the Stephenson team. We can't ask Andrew to go over."

Despite the fact that my parents were going to offer me over to the Stephenson clan—because after all, offering your worst player was a good tactical move—I really didn't care. Not when my whole body was suddenly numb. Jacob was back? When? Did Andrew know?

My brother and his ex-best friend hadn't spoken since The

Incident. I glanced toward the hallway. Toward Andrew's room. A rush of emotions flooded my system.

I forced a relaxed smile, even though my stomach felt tied into knots. "What?" I asked, wincing at the shrill pitch of my voice.

Thankfully, Mom was too busy glancing down the hallway as the ruckus grew louder. "I just wanted to warn you before we got there"—she leaned back out into the hall—"Aiden and Alex, knock it off!"

"Thanks for the warning, Mom."

Mom glanced back at me. "Yeah. At least with the quality of eighteen-year-old boys, we've got the Stephensons beat." Then she hesitated, and I waited for her to say that that was a little mean. Instead she said, "Just make sure you keep your distance. Remember what he did and how that could have ruined chances for Andrew. Boys like Jacob never change."

I stared at her, a bit shocked that she would talk about Jacob like that. Sure, he wasn't perfect. And robbing a gas station had definitely been a terrible decision on his part, but that was kind of rude.

I wanted to say something in Jacob's defense, but Mom wasn't listening anymore. She ducked out of my room, and moments later, I could hear her yelling at my brothers to clean up their room and to stop giving her grey hair.

I turned my attention back to my suitcase as I stared at my clothes. Her words rolled around in my mind. I was seeing Jacob today. Suddenly, my very well-loved and very worn sweatshirts looked horrible. There was no way Jacob could see me in these.

I closed my eyes for a moment as I let the memory of his face float through my mind. His dark hair and equally dark eyes stared back at me. He had been the resident bad boy at school. Always acting like he didn't care, but I knew better.

Jacob.

"Hey, so did Mom tell you?" My older brother Andrew asked.

Heat flushed my cheeks as I opened my eyes and glanced over at him.

"That Jacob's coming?" I shrugged as I returned to packing. I didn't want him to even remotely suspect that I was daydreaming about the friend that had deserted him.

Andrew nodded as he came over to my bed and flopped down. I could see the worry floating in his gaze. I felt bad for my brother. After Jacob and his no-good friends robbed a gas station last summer, his parents had packed him up and shipped him to Florida to spend the first semester there.

It had really affected Andrew to lose his best friend like that. And I didn't blame him. Andrew had been at the scene of the crime. Jacob had dragged him into the gas station even though he'd known what his friends were planning on doing.

I don't think Andrew ever forgave him. Even at Jacob's hearing, Andrew had remained quiet. His kept his gaze down with concern etched in his expression. I'd never seen my brother so conflicted before.

I smiled at Andrew, hoping to bolster his spirits. "It's okay. Besides, Mom said there'll be lots of games for us to play so you can slaughter Jacob in all of them."

Andrew glanced over at me, his blue eyes had turned stony. He pushed his blond hair from his face. I was eleven months younger than him, but we looked like twins.

He hesitated, but then he chuckled. "Yeah, you're right." He reached out and threw a ball of my socks into the air, catching them with one hand. "I knew I could always depend on you, Ava."

I shrugged as I grabbed the sock ball as it fell to the floor. After I tucked it back into my suitcase, I waved toward my door. "That's what sisters are for. Now, go. Pack. Mom's on the hunt." I eyed him.

He sighed and stood, wandering out of my room. "Geez, such a slave driver," he said as he disappeared down the hall.

I let out my breath as I zipped up my suitcase and wheeled it over to the door. Andrew's sentence rolled around in my mind.

I knew I could always depend on you.

Ugh. The guilt rose up in my chest.

If Andrew knew that I had a deep, irreversible crush on Jacob, he would never forgive me. What started as an innocent interest two years ago had now grown into this obnoxious obsession. I'd tried to stop liking him after everything that had gone down last summer. But my heart just wouldn't let go of Jacob's intoxicating half-smile and misunderstood demeanor.

And from the way my heart was pounding and my stomach was churning, our time apart hadn't changed anything.

Desperate for a distraction, I walked into my bathroom and grabbed my makeup, hairdryer, and the rest of my toiletries.

After they were secured in my backpack, I grabbed the handle of my suitcase and made my way to the top of the stairs.

Aiden came running out of his room, yelling as he lifted his hands to catch the football that came whizzing from the same direction. I shook my head as he glanced over at me.

"Mom's going to kill you," I said as I started down the stairs.

If Aiden heard me, it didn't stop him. He never cared. Instead, he threw the ball back to Alex and disappeared back into their room.

Once I was in the kitchen, I grabbed an apple from the nearby bowl and slipped onto a bar stool. I was ready to go, even if the rest of my family wasn't. Besides, I needed to some time to figure out how I was going to get rid of the butterflies that were dive-bombing my stomach.

I was going to see Jacob tonight, and I was in no way ready for that.

"We're here!" Dad called out in a singsong voice.

I glanced up from my book to see that Dad had pulled into the snow-cleared driveway and had turned off the car.

"Yes! We're first," Mom called out, high-fiving Dad.

I rolled my eyes. They were such dorks.

"I've gotta pee," Alex said, pushing on my seat for me to move.

I bit my tongue as choice words rushed through my mind. "Hang on," I said as I unbuckled my seatbelt and opened the side door.

In two seconds flat, Alex was out and peeing into the white snow next to the car.

"Alex! That's gross. Mom," I said, turning to stare at her.

She was too preoccupied with texting JoAnne, Jacob's mom, to punish Alex. "It's fine, honey. Besides, we haven't unlocked the cabin door yet. What else is he going to do?"

I stared at her. *Wow.* This whole competition between us and the Stephensons was getting a little absurd. Mom was now overlooking misdemeanors in favor of winning.

"Ha!" she exclaimed as Dad pulled out our luggage and set it on the ground. "They're still twenty minutes out."

Dad laughed in a triumphant manner. "Tell them that we won and they owe us pizza as a reward."

"Ooo, good idea," Mom said as she began typing on her phone.

"Are you two serious?" I asked as I grabbed my luggage.

Dad glanced over at me. "What?"

"Your son is literally peeing his name into the snow, and all you care about is winning." I waved toward Aiden who'd now joined Alex by the side of the car.

Dad glanced over and shrugged. "Your mom said it was fine, so it's fine with me."

I stared at him as I shouldered my backpack. What was happening to my parents? I shook my head. "I'm going inside."

Dad handed the keys to me as I walked past him. Once inside, I turned on the lights.

It was a fully furnished cabin. My parents had paid for the

RULE #4 YOU CAN'T MISINTERPRET A MISTLETOE KISS | 7

deluxe package, which included all of the Christmas trimmings. I glanced at the ten-foot decorated tree that sat next to the fireplace. The ornaments glittered and the tinsel shimmered in the setting sun. Garland was wrapped around the banister that ran up to the second floor. Mistletoe hung over the opening to the kitchen.

"Wow, this is amazing," Mom said as she stepped in behind me.

I glanced over at her. Ever since Dad got the promotion over Dirk Stephenson, they had no problem flashing money around. They had insisted that they pay for the cabin when they asked the Stephensons to join us this year.

When they first planned the trip, spending Christmas vacation with them seemed like a good idea. I mean, the Stephensons were nice. Besides Jacob, they had a daughter, Tracy, who was two years younger than me, and a seven-year-old adopted son, Max. Alex and Aiden loved Max, and they were always terrorizing me and Tracy. Things were simple if Jacob wasn't involved. But now that he was coming, I wasn't sure I liked any of this.

"You did a good job, Mom," I said as I moved toward the stairs. "I'm guessing Tracy and I are sharing a room?"

Mom nodded. "Yep. Should be the last door down the hall."

I nodded as I climbed the stairs, my suitcase banging on each step. I found the smallest room and walked inside. There was a single bunkbed, which was pushed up against the wall. I grabbed my luggage and began to unpack my clothes, slipping them into the rustic dresser.

We were staying here for the next five days, so I might as well get comfortable. After setting out my stuff on half of the dresser, I grabbed my pillow and shook out the blanket on the bottom bed. Tracy would probably appreciate the top bunk, plus, I was getting a bit too old to be climbing up and down the ladder to get into bed.

"They're here!" Mom called out, her voice carrying through the open bedroom door.

My heart picked up speed as I went to the window and glanced down. The Stephensons were out of their van and walking up the driveway. I tried to keep my gaze from falling on Jacob, but it was like I was a homing pigeon. I couldn't help but stare at him.

His hair was longer now. He pushed his hands through it as he listened to something his mom was saying. He nodded, and I couldn't help but notice how tan he'd gotten in the six months he'd been gone.

He glanced up to my window, and heat rushed through my body as I collapsed to the floor, praying he hadn't seen me.

I took a few deep breaths, hoping to still the embarrassment that had my head swimming. What the heck was I doing? What was wrong with me?

I needed to stop liking Jacob. Besides, what was I going to tell Andrew? He was my brother and my best friend. I needed to be loyal to him no matter how much my stomach lightened at the thought of seeing Jacob again.

"Ava! Andrew! Come down and says hi to the Stephensons. They graciously brought us dinner," Mom called.

I sighed. This was going to be a long vacation. I wasn't sure how much longer I could pretend to care who won their ridiculous holiday competition. And spending every minute of every day around Jacob was the last thing I needed to help me keep my resolve to stop liking him.

What a holly, jolly Christmas for me.

CHAPTER TWO

I padded down the stairs, trying to look relaxed even though I felt like a mess inside. What was I going to do when I saw Jacob again? Did I shake his hand? Give him a hug?

I shook my head, forcing that last option from my mind. I didn't need to be putting ridiculous ideas in my head. What if I accidentally acted on them? I cringed.

Stupid. Stupid thoughts.

As soon as I got to the bottom step, I took a deep breath. I could do this. I was the only one privy to my absurd crush. No one else knew. And if I was smart, no one would ever find out.

I'd survive this Christmas getaway and then move on with my life. I just needed to keep my head down and not totally embarrass myself.

Both families were in the kitchen when I walked in. I tucked my blonde hair behind my ears as I glanced around. Thankfully, no one really noticed that I was there.

I scanned the room, but didn't find Jacob. Where had he gone?

Andrew and Tracy were leaning against the island, consumed with something on their phones. Max, Aiden, and Alex were sitting at the table, eating pizza. And Mr. Stephenson and Dad were arm wrestling at the counter. I glanced over at Mom, who was cheering Dad on. Both men were red-faced and squinting with effort.

After picking up a piece of cheese pizza, I slipped over to the corner behind the cupboards. Just as I stepped into hiding, I heard a low chuckle, and a hand pressed against my lower back.

"Whoa," Jacob's low, smooth voice said.

Heat instantly flushed my body. So this was where Jacob had disappeared to. I slowly turned around, trying to still my pounding heart when I met his dark brown eyes, crinkled from his half-smile.

What was I supposed to say? Hi, how's it going? I've been in love with you for three years? I pinched my lips, refusing to let any of those words out. Was I having a brain aneurism? Because it felt as if nothing inside of my head made sense.

He raised his eyebrows as he studied me.

Say something, you idiot!

"Hey," I breathed. Great. That's the best thing I could come up with?

Jacob's half-smile was back. "It's good to see you, Ava."

I stared at him. Did he really mean that? And then common sense caught up with me. It was a totally normal greeting, not a declaration of love.

"You, too."

There was a cheer from around the corner. I glanced over to see Mr. Stephenson pump his fists into the air, grab a piece of supreme pizza, and triumphantly take a bite.

I glanced back at Jacob. He didn't look too interested in what was happening. Instead, he picked off a few peppers from his slice and stacked them on his plate.

"What was that about?" I asked, taking a bite of my pizza.

Jacob glanced up and shrugged. "They're dumb. Something about wanting the last piece of supreme pizza."

I snorted. Yep, that sounded about right. "It's so weird, huh?" I asked, leaning against the cupboard.

Jacob shook his head. "They're an embarrassment." He shoved the last bite of crust into his mouth and crumpled up his paper plate. He stepped past me and made his way over to the garbage.

I tried not to stare at him, I really did. But I couldn't help it. Sure, he'd gotten in trouble, and he played like he didn't care about anything, but I knew that was all an act. I took a bite of my pizza as Andrew glanced over at me, his eyebrows furrowed.

I knew he was wondering about my conversation with Jacob. I shrugged as I motioned toward the alcove that was rapidly becoming my favorite place in the house.

Andrew nodded and straightened as he walked over to me. "What did you talk to Jacob about?" he asked, slipping his phone into his pocket and folding his arms.

"Not much. Just how annoying our parents are." I took another bite and reveled in the memory of talking to Jacob. Why did I have to like him as much as I did?

"That's it?"

I glanced over at Andrew. "Yeah. That's it. Why? Did you want us to talk about something else?"

Andrew's lips drew into a tight line before he sighed. "No. Not really."

I eyed my brother. Why was he acting so strange? He was over six feet tall. He was quarter back on the football team with a full-ride scholarship to UC. Nothing ever rattled him like this.

"Is there a certain topic you want us to discuss next time I talk to him?" A shiver raced across my skin. There was going to be a next time? And then I felt stupid. Of course, there would be. We were staying in the same house. There was bound to be a reason to talk to each other again.

Andrew shoved his hands through his hair as he shook his head. "I just wish he hadn't come," he said, his voice low.

I reached out and patted his arm. "I know. But you guys were friends once. I'm sure you can find it in your heart to be friends again." I brushed off my mouth and crumpled my plate—sadly without the same finesse as Jacob. I grinned at Andrew. "Besides, it's Christmas—the most magical time of the year."

He scoffed and shook his head. "I doubt that will have any impact on our friendship."

I shrugged and started walking over toward the garbage, where I disposed of my plate. "Don't write it off." I winked at my brother and headed out of the kitchen.

I took a deep breath and let it out slowly. I could do this. I could survive this trip.

When I walked into the living room, I found a giant whiteboard had been set up against the wall. My parents and the Stephensons were busy writing on it and talking.

I glanced at what they were listing.

Christmas Tree Decorating

Cookie Decorating

Ice Fishing

Mom was in the process of writing *Gift Wrapping* when I cleared my throat.

"What are you doing?" I asked.

Mom glanced over at me. "We're making a list. We are going to show the world how much Christmas spirit we have."

I stared at her. "You can't be serious, Mom. It's all to win the vacation? Isn't it time to let some of this ridiculous competition stuff go?"

Mom laughed and was joined by Mrs. Stephenson a moment later.

"Come on, Ava. It's all in good fun," Mrs. Stephenson said. Her bright red lips smiled at me. "Plus, we could really use a vacation." It seemed like she was trying to be relaxed, but I could see the stress permeating off of her.

Not sure what to do with that, I just glanced between her and my mom and then shook my head. "You two are crazy," I said.

"Crazy enough to win," Mom said as she turned and finished writing.

I sat down on the recliner and pulled my feet underneath me. There was no way I was going to participate in this, but there was also no way I was going to miss the show.

My parents were weird in an *I can't stop staring even though it burns my eyes* kind of way. While they finished figuring out the scoring for the items on the board, I grabbed a nearby book and flipped through it.

My ears perked up when they began to discuss the fact that the teams were uneven. I wanted to see how fast my parents would "graciously" offer to give me over to the Stephensons. And if I were honest, I was really hoping the Stephensons said yes.

"Well, you guys just weren't as *busy* as we were. We shouldn't be punished for that," Dad said, wrapping his arm around Mom and nuzzling her neck.

Bleh. I did not want to hear *that*. There was nothing worse than hearing your parents talk about the birds and the bees. I closed my eyes, forcing that disturbing image far, far, into the depths of my mind.

"Well, there's nothing we can do about that now," Mrs. Stephenson said. I could hear the bite to her tone. There was a reason Max was adopted, and I had a feeling Dad hit a nerve with his comment.

"Of course," Mom's apologetic voice piped up. "You can have…"

I paused, holding my breath.

"Ava."

I pinched my lips together as I stared really hard at a page in the book that had a picture of a lighthouse on it.

"Ava?" Mrs. Stephenson asked. From the corner of my eye, I saw her turn to study me. She sighed. "I guess."

I tried to ignore the fact that she sounded less than thrilled. I'm sure she wanted Andrew, but I was at least better than my hooligan younger brothers, even if I had no skills to write home about.

"Perfect. It's settled then."

I bit my lip, trying to sort through my emotions. I was going to spend the entire time here hanging out with Jacob. Even though it felt perfect, I was worried. How was I going to keep my feelings at bay when I literally needed to spend every moment with him?

Ten minutes later, we were all called to meet in the living room.

Andrew and Jacob sat on opposite ends of the couch. One would have never guessed those two had been best friends for most their lives. They had their arms folded and were looking anywhere but at each other.

Tracy smiled as she sat down in the armchair next to me, her camera hanging from her neck. She pushed up her glasses. "What's this about?" she asked.

I glanced over at her and then waved toward the whiteboard. "Our crazy parents. Won't even take a break for the holidays."

She moved to study the board and then shook her head. "Every year," she muttered under her breath.

The three rowdy boys began wrestling on the floor in front of the fireplace, getting close enough to the tree to almost knock it down. Mom and Mrs. Stephenson yelled at them to sit still.

After everything settled down, Dad clapped his hands like he was a school teacher.

"This year we've decided to enter into the Little Foot Christmas competition," he said, grinning from ear to ear as if this was *the* coolest thing any parent had ever done ever.

"So we've planned a bunch of Christmas activities. We need to take pictures of the finished products as well as the process. According to them, it's not only the end product that counts, but the journey we take to get to the finish line." He rolled his eyes.

"So, it's not only important for you to do well," he continued, "but to make sure you look happy while you're doing it."

RULE #4 YOU CAN'T MISINTERPRET A MISTLETOE KISS | 15

There was a collective groan.

Dad waved his hand. "None of that. If you want Christmas presents, you will participate."

No one groaned at that.

Dad smiled. *Great.* My parents had resorted to threats. Suddenly, this whole thing felt less Christmasy and more like a mafia movie.

Mr. Stephenson joined Dad as they described the different competitions. They waved away Tracy's question about why we were doing two more Christmas trees. It was all part of their master plan to get us into the spirit, they said. How they saw pitting people against each other to win a prize as getting into the Christmas spirit was beyond me. But they wouldn't let up. We were doing this. No matter what.

After the rules were explained, and Tracy was assigned to take pictures, we spilt up into our respective groups. My legs had fallen asleep, so I tried not to wince as I hobbled over to the Stephensons, who'd agreed to meet in the kitchen.

The only open spot at the table was right next to Jacob. Let me repeat myself. Right. Next. To. Jacob.

I swallowed as I made my way over, hoping I didn't look like a jumble of nerves.

I pulled out my chair, and Jacob glanced over at me. His smile caused my cheeks to burn. This was not good. Oh, this was *not* good.

"Glad you can join us," Mrs. Stephenson said once I was situated.

"Happy to be here," I said, smiling over at her.

Her expression grew serious as she leaned toward me. "I want you to swear, right now, that you are not going to tell our secrets to your family." She leaned in closer. "Swear?"

"Geez, Mom," Jacob said and then glanced over at me. "Don't listen to her. She doesn't mean it."

I nodded at him and then over to Mrs. Stephenson. "I swear.

You're my team now. We're going to beat them." I gave her my best game face, and that seemed to appease her.

She straightened and nodded. "That's right. We are. Now, let's talk tree decorating." She rubbed her temples. "We have until tomorrow morning to produce our best Christmas tree ever." She glanced over at Mr. Stephenson. "I say, you, Max, Tracy, and I head to the store for decorations. Ava and Jacob?"

We both turned our attention to her.

"Can you two manage the tree?" She paused. "I mean, Ava, you pick out the tree. Jacob, you carry it." Then she leaned forward. "If you ruin this for us…" She let her voice trail off as she studied him.

Jacob met her gaze with equal intensity. But then he sighed and slumped in his chair. "It's just a dumb tree. There's no way even I can ruin it."

She stared at him for a moment longer before she nodded. "Great." Then she glanced over at Mr. Stephenson. "Ready?"

Mr. Stephenson directed those going to the store to get their shoes on and meet at the car in ten minutes.

When the kitchen was emptied of everyone be me and Jacob, I peeked over at him. His arms were folded and his jaw set. I didn't blame him. His mom had been unnecessarily harsh to him. I'd be mad as well.

"Are you okay with this?" I asked, waving toward myself. Then I winced. What if he said no? How would that make me feel? I braced myself for his answer.

Jacob scoffed and then shoved his hands into his front pockets. "If you mean this ridiculous competition, then no. If you mean hanging you with you? Then…maybe." He shot me a smile as he headed toward the stairs. "Meet you down here in five."

I stared as his retreating frame, trying to dissect what he had just said. What did "maybe" mean?

CHAPTER THREE

I tried to forget what Jacob said and how he said it, while I slipped into my snow pants and boots. I was still trying to forget while I put on my coat, gloves, and hat.

By the time I was finished, I'd spent more time trying to forget what we'd talked about than we'd actually spent talking to each other. What a perfect start to our time together.

My stomach was twisted, and my thoughts were so tangled up that I felt as if I were drowning in the ocean of my mind.

I stood by the back door, waiting for Jacob. Noise behind me drew my attention, and I raised an eyebrow as he approached.

"That's what you're wearing?" I asked, eyeing his leather jacket and boots.

No snow pants. No hat. No gloves. He looked like he was heading out on a motorcycle ride instead of trudging through the Colorado snow in search of a tree.

Jacob glanced over at me and smirked. "It's better than you. You look like the kid from *A Christmas Story*. Typical Ava. Always going overboard."

I stared at him and then down to my outer wear. How was this going overboard?

"I do not," I said.

Blast. My cheeks were burning. Why did he have to say that? Now I was totally self-conscious.

"And I don't go overboard." My voice was high and squeaky.

Jacob ran his gaze over me again as he leaned back. "Jury's in, and yes, you do."

I glared at him. "Well, at least *I'm* not going to freeze," I said, trudging past him and opening the back door.

I made my way down the steps and over to the shed out back. Mrs. Stephenson said that there was an axe stored there. I had a lot of doubts about our ability to cut down a whole tree with just an axe, but Mrs. Stephenson blew off my concerns with the wave of her hand.

The sound of crunching snow signaled that Jacob was following me. I kept my gaze forward, refusing to let myself look behind me. I was a little upset that he'd teased me like that. After all the times I'd defended him in my mind when my parents talked about how bad he was, this was how he treated me?

Of course I'd never said any of those things out loud, but still.

I swung open the shed door and found the axe. I slung it over my shoulder like I'd seen people do in the old-timey movies I loved to watch.

"Whoa," Jacob said, holding up his hands when he saw the axe.

I glared at him. "I've got it," I said.

Jacob's eyebrows went up as he studied me. "Are you upset?" he asked.

Not wanting to admit that I actually cared about what he'd said to me, I shrugged and started off through the snow. The prime Christmas tree spot was twenty minutes away. The sun was already low in the sky, and I did not want to be stuck out here in the freezing cold when it got dark.

"Hey, Ava," Jacob called, his voice growing louder as he caught up with me.

I hesitated, wanting to turn around, but then I kept moving.

"Hey," he said, grabbing my elbow and halting me.

Glancing back at him, I swallowed. His normal cocky smile was gone, and his brows were furrowed. Did he feel bad for what he'd said?

"What?" I asked. My breath came out in long white wisps.

Jacob's nose, cheeks, and tips of his ears were red.

"I'm sorry that you took what I said as an insult," he said as he dropped his shoulders and shoved his hands into his front pockets.

I studied him. Was he serious? He was *blaming* me for getting upset? "Jacob, what the heck? Was that supposed to be an apology?"

He studied me as if he were surprised. "It was," he said.

I pinched my lips shut and turned away from him. "Come on. Let's go get the tree, then I can teach you the proper way to apologize."

It didn't take long for Jacob to fall into step with me. We walked a few minutes in silence before I saw him turn to study me.

"I think I understand what I did wrong," he said.

I snorted as I glanced toward the edge of the forest in front of us. "You do?"

He nodded. "You're upset that I said you looked like a little boy who can't put his arms down. And when I apologized, I didn't admit I was wrong. Instead I basically told you it was your fault for being offended."

"Ding, ding, ding." I exclaimed as I glanced over at him. "We have a winner!"

He pulled back a little, looking surprised.

I dropped my gaze. "Sorry. Sarcasm is one of my many faults—or so my mom tells me." I shifted the axe around on my shoulder. It was starting to dig into my skin.

"Can I?" he asked, nodding toward the axe.

I hesitated and then nodded as I lowered it to the ground. In a swift movement, he pulled it up and rested it on his shoulder as if it weighed nothing. I couldn't help but stare. How strong had he gotten?

"What?" he asked.

My stomach flipped as I turned and shrugged. "Nothing."

We walked a bit farther before he spoke again.

"I don't think that was nothing, Ava. You were staring. Why?"

When I glanced over at him, he winked at me.

"I wasn't—I mean—You've—" With every attempt, his eyebrows rose higher. I growled as I headed through the snow. "You're impossible," I said.

Suddenly, he wasn't this mysterious, sexy ex-best friend of my brother's. Now, he was just an annoying boy who had me all discombobulated.

"You're really rattled," he said as he caught up with me.

"I am?" I asked, glancing over at him. "Well, it must be the lack of oxygen. Or the fact that I'm stuck tromping through the snow with you to get a tree so our parents can compete for a vacation. This whole thing is insane." I tried to think just what my parents were always fighting the Stephensons for, but nothing came to mind, and that just frustrated me further. "Why are we constantly battling each other?"

Jacob walked over to me and patted my shoulder. Even though there were layers of clothing between his skin and mine, my whole body tingled from his touch.

"Calm down, Ava. I didn't mean to rile you up." He gave me a small smile. One that I'd seen only a few times before. It was Jacob's genuine smile. The one that made him look like a good person, instead of the delinquent he tried to convince everyone he was.

I took a deep breath and let it out slowly as I studied him. Wow. I was a complete emotional basket case. Maybe this was the reason I'd never had a boyfriend before. I needed to chill.

When he was sure that I was okay, he dropped his hand and motioned toward the forest. "Shall we?" he asked.

Fearful of what might come out of my mouth, I just nodded, and fell into step beside him. Now that I had sufficiently embarrassed myself, I peeked over at him.

"I'm sorry," I whispered.

He chuckled. It was low and melodious. "You don't have to apologize, Ava. You're right. Sometimes I tease when I get uncomfortable."

I couldn't help but stare at him. He actually sounded sincere.

"You're staring again," he said, not looking up to meet my gaze.

I turned my attention to the snow. "Sorry. I guess I've never heard you be so honest before." I shut my mouth as my last words fell around me. He'd been honest with me, and yet here I was, insulting him again.

When he fell silent, I looked over at him.

"If you want to know something, you should just ask," he said as we approached the small grove of Christmas trees that the cabin owners had planted. It was the same grove our current Christmas tree had come from.

How much did I want to ask? Would he be truthful? My parents had been pretty thorough in telling us about his crime and how we should watch who we associate with. Andrew had been so upset he didn't speak a word in defense of his friend or in frustration. He was just silent. Even Aiden and Alex had asked questions.

"About last summer?" I asked, letting the question slip from my lips before I thought about the repercussions.

He hesitated as he stopped next to a short, plump tree. Its branches were so full you could barely see through to the other side. It was perfect.

"That one," I said, nodding toward it.

Jacob studied the trunk before he raised the axe and started striking through the bark. I winced with each blow, wondering how Jacob had enough strength to deliver them.

He paused after he was about a quarter of the way through, resting the axe on the ground. He glanced over at me. "So? What do you want to know?"

I eyed him. "Well…" Where did I start?

He gave me a look as he slipped off his coat and handed it to me. I tried to ignore how well he filled out the dark blue shirt he had on underneath. His cheeks were pink, but I had a feeling it was more from exertion than the cold.

"Why did you do it?" That seemed like a good place to start.

He pinched his lips together, and it seemed as if he was choosing his words. Then his shoulders relaxed as he met my gaze. "Don't you know? That's just my nature."

I parted my lips. Was he serious? There was no way that was true. There was something else going on here, and I was going to figure it out.

His brow furrowed as he gave me one last look, and then he picked up the axe and started on the tree again. All my arguments against his response left me as I watched him. His arm flexed when he struck the trunk, to help control the shock that was radiating up the handle.

A look of determination passed over his face as he pulled the axe back and concentrated on the place he wanted to hit. Only Jacob could make a mundane task like this look incredibly sexy. I didn't want to leave our conversation where it had stopped, but I also didn't want him to stop chopping down the tree. I was so torn.

Feeling a bit guilty for just standing there, staring, I dropped my gaze and focused on my gloved hands. I would figure out my response for after we'd collected the tree.

Suddenly, two hands grabbed me and pulled me to the side. I stumbled over my feet, and the ground rushed toward me. Just before I disappeared into the powdery snow, Jacob threw himself underneath me.

The snow puffed up around us as I landed on top of him. My hands sprawled across his chest as he winced from the impact. I was mortified.

"What are you doing?" I asked once I found my voice.

He glanced up at me. I was keenly aware of the pressure of his hands wrapped around my upper arms and even more aware of his very-toned body underneath me.

I was on top of Jacob. I tried not to freak out as I wiggled around, trying to get up. I needed to get away from him. Laying on top of a boy I was trying very hard not to like didn't seem like the best idea.

Jacob chuckled as he let go of my arms and helped me to stand.

"If you hadn't been zoning out, you would have heard me yell, 'timber,'" he said as he sat up, resting his arms on his knees.

I wanted to melt under his playful gaze. He looked pretty pleased with himself.

I brushed the snow from my legs and glanced over at him. "I didn't hear anything," I said.

He shrugged as he moved to stand. Then he walked over to the tree that had landed right where I was standing.

"Proof, Miss Rogers."

I glanced at him and then down to the tree that had almost smushed me. I sighed as I shot him a smile. "Well…why did you let it fall there?"

He scoffed as he grabbed the axe and swung it up onto his shoulder. Then he reached down and grabbed one of the lower branches. The tree left a trail in the snow as he began dragging it back to the house. Just as he passed by me, he made a point to pause inches from my face.

"That wasn't intentional," he said. His voice was low and meaningful. His gaze met mine, and my heart literally stuttered in my chest.

"I...um...thanks," I finally managed.

He held my gaze before he winked. "Anything for a teammate," he said as he turned and started making his way back to the house.

I was so confused by what had happened. I followed behind him, keeping the length of the tree between us. I needed a moment to dissect how I felt about all of this.

CHAPTER FOUR

*E*veryone had returned from their shopping by the time we got back to the cabin. They were all buzzing around, talking and laughing, which made it easy to put some space between me and Jacob.

I needed a moment to figure out where I stood on the feelings that were now coursing through me. I kept to the far end of the kitchen, watching everyone else swarm the trees that were now propped up in the living room. Tracy was moving around, snapping pictures. She made her way into the kitchen and then stopped in front of me and raised her camera.

I gave her a small smile, and after she took the picture, she glanced at me and left.

"Ava, dear, grab the lights from the paper bag and meet me in the living room," Mrs. Stephenson called from behind the tree. I could see her blonde hair poking up above its branches.

I sighed as I folded my arms and leaned against the counter. My thoughts were still concentrated on Jacob, and these few minutes of quiet hadn't been enough to cure me of the feelings that were bubbling up inside.

But Mrs. Stephenson didn't seem to care. She came barreling

through the kitchen and held up her fingers, motioning me toward the living room.

There were five paper bags all lined up beside me. After looking through them all, I found three boxes of twinkle lights and pulled them out. By the time I got to the tree, Mrs. Stephenson was circling it like a hungry wolf.

"This is truly a spectacular tree," she said as she glanced over at me with an appreciative gaze.

I shrugged and waved toward Jacob, who was staring at his phone as he leaned against the far wall. "Jacob was the one who found it," I said.

Mrs. Stephenson glanced over to Jacob, and I could tell she wanted to say something, but she stopped herself. Instead, she just smiled at me and tilted her head toward my parents, who were unwrapping their tree from its netting.

"Our freshly cut tree is heads above their store-bought one," she said.

Dad turned around. "We bought ours from the Cub Scouts outside Sid's Hardware. We helped support a local troop. You"—Dad pointed his finger at us—"destroyed a squirrel's home."

I rolled my eyes. What were we, the Bearstein bears? "Okay, Dad."

Mrs. Stephenson snorted, and as the branches of my family's tree began to settle down, she turned to me with a huge smile. "Do you see the bare spots?" she asked, holding up her hand and pointing at her palm in a sad attempt to ,ask the fact that she was mocking my parents' tree.

Dad did not look happy as he circled their tree. Something must have gone wrong during the transportation because one side was missing about half of its needles.

Mr. And Mrs. Stephenson high-fived and then moved around to celebrate with the rest of the team. I obliged them, slapping their hands with moderate enthusiasm. Jacob didn't even try. He just left his mom hanging there.

Mrs. Stephenson waited for a few seconds before she moved on to Max.

I waited for everyone to engross themselves in stringing lights before I made my way over to Jacob. I leaned against the wall, waiting for him to acknowledge me. When he didn't, I peeked over his shoulder to see that he was playing Candy Crush.

I chuckled. He did not seem like the kind of guy who enjoyed that game.

"What?" he asked, not looking up.

I shrugged. "I guess I didn't see you as the Candy Crush kind of guy," I said as I folded my arms across my chest.

Noise drew my attention over to my family. Aiden was whining at Mom as he held up his favorite Lego guy, and Mom was telling him that the Lego was not an appropriate Christmas decoration. Aiden pushed out his lip as he stomped over to the chair. I shot him a sympathetic look, but he just covered his face with a nearby pillow.

I found Jacob studying me when I turned my attention back to him. Our eyes met for a brief moment before he turned his attention back to his phone.

"So, what kind of games does a *guy like me* play?" he asked.

I was a little taken back by the intensity of his gaze. What was he thinking? I swallowed as I focused on his question. "I don't know, *Grand Theft Auto*?" Truth was, I really didn't know too many video games.

He paused before he snorted. "Yeah. Because only a delinquent like me would play a game about stealing stuff." He pressed the power button, and his phone's screen went dark. He shot me a look, which I couldn't quite interpret, and pushed off the wall. Just as he stepped away from me, Mrs. Stephenson waved at us.

"Good, you're done with your phone. I want you and Ava to go to the kitchen, pop some popcorn, and get started stringing. We are going for a rustic feel."

Mrs. Stephenson turned back to the lights and resumed arguing with Mr. Stephenson about placement.

My parents were engrossed with their tree on the other side of the room, so I turned to Jacob. He had a strained expression. Great. He did not look like someone who wanted to spend an evening stringing popcorn with me.

I shrugged as I moved passed him. "You can just go. I'm a pretty good threader. I'll have this done in no time." I didn't look back as I made my way into the kitchen. I didn't want to find out if he had or hadn't followed me. Living in the hazy fog of denial sounded pretty good right now.

I located the popcorn in one of the grocery bags and began pulling off the plastic to get them ready for the microwave. Just as I opened the door to stick a bag in, I caught Jacob's reflection in the glass.

He *had* followed me. He'd come to help. *Whoa. Easy on the butterflies, stomach.*

I tried not to seem surprised as I slipped the bag in and started the timer. I slowly turned around and rested my hand on the counter. We stood in silence for a few moments. I wondered if he would start talking or if he was waiting for me to say something.

Just as I moved to speak, Andrew walked in.

An icy feeling instantly filled the air. I glanced between Jacob and my brother, wondering what exactly had happened. Sure, Jacob had basically chosen a life of crime over a friendship with Andrew, but why did they hate each other so much?

"Sorry to intrude," Andrew said, moving to stand next to me like I was a human shield or something.

I shrugged, giving him an encouraging smile. Whatever had happened between the two of them, they could get over it. I was pretty sure that forgiveness was something my brother could handle. "It's fine. We're..." I trailed off before I gave away our decorating secrets. I wrinkled my nose. "Wait a minute, you are the enemy," I said as I elbowed Andrew in the ribs.

RULE #4 YOU CAN'T MISINTERPRET A MISTLETOE KISS | 29

Andrew chuckled, and from the corner of my eye, I saw Jacob's jaw tighten. What was with him? He was the one who hurt my brother, not the other way around.

Deciding to ignore Jacob's reaction, I turned back to Andrew. "So, what are you doing in here—besides spying on us?"

Andrew seemed to relax as he reached out and grabbed a caramel from the bowl on the counter. After unwrapping it, he stuck it in his mouth and chewed thoughtfully. "Well, I am the best at getting the truth from people," he said.

Jacob scoffed, drawing our attention. When he noticed we were staring at him, he shrugged as he pulled out his phone and started playing on it again.

I glanced over at Andrew, whose face had reddened. I furrowed my brow. That was a strange reaction. But before I could ask about it, Andrew met my gaze and rolled his eyes.

I wasn't sure what was going on between my brother and Jacob, but I was pretty sure I wasn't going to figure it out here in the kitchen.

As soon as the microwave beeped, I turned, grateful for the distraction. I pressed the release button and gingerly grabbed the steaming bag. "Seriously though, Andrew, you have to leave. You and I can't be seen talking to each other. It's ridiculous, but Mrs. Stephenson thinks that you'll steal her ideas." Plus, I was ready to get Andrew moving.

I loved my brother, but he was blocking me from Jacob. And I wasn't joking about Mrs. Stephenson. If she saw me consorting with the enemy…well, I wasn't sure what she would do to me exactly, but it wouldn't be pretty.

Andrew shrugged as he grabbed a handful of popcorn from the bowl I was pouring it into. I protested, but he just smiled and headed out of the kitchen.

Once he was gone, the room seemed to relax again. I glanced over toward Jacob, wondering how to get him to talk to me, then yelped when I saw him standing right next to me with another bag of popcorn in hand.

"Wha—you're—" I pinched my lips together and forced myself to stop talking.

"I figured you needed some help," he said, glancing over at me with one of his million-watt smiles spread across his face.

Too stunned to speak, I just nodded.

We popped popcorn and filled the bowl in a surprisingly comfortable silence. Before I knew it, the metal bowl was overflowing with popcorn.

"Ready to start stringing?" he asked, grabbing the bowl and nodding toward the kitchen table.

I found the needles and thread and followed after him. He took the chair that was tucked under the short end of the table, and I grabbed the chair right next to it. We were sitting inches apart.

I hated how my heart rate picked up from being so close to him. There was no way I was going to survive this vacation with how fast blood was pumping through my body. I was pretty sure my heart would just give up at some point.

Ready to distract myself, I decided to break the silence.

"So, what's with you and my brother?" I kept my gaze focused on the thread that I was unwinding from the spool. I knew this was probably a testy subject for him, but I couldn't handle the awkward feeling between him and my brother if we were going to be stuck in the same house.

When Jacob didn't answer, I peered over at him. His jaw was set and he was staring hard at the popcorn piece in front of him.

"It's okay, you don't have to tell me," I said.

Jacob glanced over at me, and for the first time, I saw pain there. It was so strong that it was almost palpable. He was hurt.

But, just as quickly as that look had come, it disappeared. He shrugged as he picked up some popcorn and popped it into his

RULE #4 YOU CAN'T MISINTERPRET A MISTLETOE KISS | 31

mouth. "Just a falling out, I guess," he said as he broke open the package of needles and pulled one out.

Once I had a long piece of string, I handed the spool over to him, and he did the same. Soon, we were threading the popcorn.

Desperate to redeem myself, I changed topics. "How was your grandmother's?"

Jacob's shoulders relaxed, and I knew I'd picked a good subject.

I sat there, stringing popcorn, as I listened to Jacob. He talked about the school he went to, his classmates, and the ocean. A lot about the ocean.

It was like he was a different person, hearing him talk like this. In all my life, I'd never gotten him to share this much. It was either something he really cared about, or he was just grateful to not talk about Andrew and their falling out.

Either way, I loved it. I loved the fact that he felt relaxed enough to talk to me. Growing up, it had always been Andrew that he talked to—not me. But now, that was different. I seemed to be the only person in the house that he wanted to talk to.

And while I was trying not to read too much into that, I couldn't help it. I couldn't help but think that he was talking to me because he wanted to. That I had something special to offer him.

Though I knew that made me seem like the biggest idiot in the world.

CHAPTER FIVE

Once we were done stringing popcorn, Mrs. Stephenson came in, declared our work adequate, and ushered us out to the living room to start decorating the tree. I giggled as Jacob got trapped between the tree and the popcorn string.

He made a face which caused me to laugh harder—to the annoyance of Mrs. Stephenson.

When we finally got him untangled, I glanced over at my parents' tree to see Andrew studying us. His eyebrows were furrowed, and he was glaring at Jacob.

My laughter died down as I watched him. What was with him? From the way my parents and the Stephensons were moving around the living room, no one else seemed to notice the heavy air between them.

Maybe it was just me. Maybe I was making it into a bigger deal than it was.

After the popcorn was wrapped around the tree, Mom declared that it was time to break for dinner.

We all filed into the kitchen, where Mom had been cooking a roast in the crockpot. After everyone dished up, I went and sat

RULE #4 YOU CAN'T MISINTERPRET A MISTLETOE KISS | 33

down at the table. To my frustration, Andrew joined me, taking the only open chair next to me.

I peeked over at Jacob, who had been heading over. But he stopped once Andrew settled in. Instead of sitting at the opposite end of the table, he grabbed a soda and slipped into the living room.

Now I'd not only missed an opportunity to sit next to Jacob, but he was nowhere to be seen. *Thanks, Andrew.*

Trying to make the best of this situation, I glanced over at my brother, who was shoveling the roast beef into his mouth. I pulled a disgusted expression as I cut my potato into smaller bites.

Aiden and Alex were busy throwing their carrots at each other, and Mom was scolding them. For some reason, when Jacob wasn't here, the magic of this vacation was sucked out of me. I was back to being plain, ol' Ava. And nothing very special ever happened to her.

I studied my brother. He glanced over at me and shrugged.

"What?" he asked through a mouthful of meat.

I shook my head and turned my attention back to my plate. "Nothing," I said as I pushed my food around. Suddenly, I wasn't very hungry.

And then I decided to confront the person who was causing this lack of an appetite. My brother.

Sure, Jacob didn't want to tell me the truth, but Andrew would. He was my blood relative. I was sure there was a law that, as siblings, you must tell each other the truth.

"What's with you and Jacob?" I asked, taking a bite of my potato.

Andrew coughed and grabbed his glass of water. After a long drink, he set his cup down and glanced over at me. "What did Jacob say?" he asked. There was an accusatory hint to his voice.

I eyed him, then I shook my head. "Nothing. Seriously. He's shut up tighter than a clam about you." I dipped a piece of meat into some gravy and slipped it into my mouth. It almost melted when it hit my tongue.

Say what you want about Mom, but she knew how to make a mean roast.

"He hasn't told you anything?" Andrew asked. He sounded relieved.

I studied him. "Nope. Nothing," I said, drawing out each word. So there *was* something. "What shouldn't he be telling me?"

Andrew shrugged as he zeroed in on his vegetables. After he finished half of them, he turned his attention back over to me. "Jacob believes things happened differently that night last summer." He downed the rest of his water. "He hates me because of it."

I stared at Andrew. "He blames you for the fact that he robbed a gas station?" I knit my eyebrows together. That didn't make sense. I didn't know a lot about Jacob, but I did know he wasn't delusional. Why would he assume Andrew had anything to do with it?

After scooping up the rest of his food, Andrew set his fork down on his plate and stood. "I don't know, Ava. He's crazy. Don't believe anything he tells you about me."

Frustration rose up in my stomach. I did not like the fact that my brother was calling Jacob crazy. Sure, he was mysterious and brooding in a sexy kind of way…wait, where was I going with this?

I blinked a few times, trying to get my thoughts together. But before I could respond to Andrew's allegations, he was already out of earshot. I watched as he dumped his dishes into the sink and made his way out of the kitchen, stating that he was headed upstairs to get some of his honors homework done.

Mom started to protest, but Andrew reminded her that if she wanted him to keep his scholarship, he needed to do his school work. That seemed to appease Mom, and after one look at the Stephensons, she nodded.

RULE #4 YOU CAN'T MISINTERPRET A MISTLETOE KISS | 35

I could see her thoughts written across her face. She wanted Andrew to win at the *get into college and come out with the best job* game they were playing with the Stephensons. My stomach churned at the thought. This competition was really getting out of hand. Both sets of parents were being terrible role models.

Not wanting my food anymore, I stood, grabbed my plate, dumped the remaining food into the garbage, and set it by the sink. After drying my hands, I moved out into the living room.

As I left, I overheard the parents discussing how it might be a good idea to give the kids some time to relax. They'd start up the competition again tomorrow morning.

I tried to keep my gaze trained on the ground as I walked past Jacob, who had finished his food and was back on his phone.

I tried to force my feet over to the stairs so that I could hide out in my room and figure out how I felt about everything that had happened today, but they didn't comply. Instead, I found myself over at the bookshelf, pulling out a book and sitting down in the armchair across from Jacob.

I flipped open the book I'd picked, *A Christmas Carol*, and started reading it.

It was a tradition I'd started a few years ago—I would read *A Christmas Carol* during the week of Christmas. It was stupid, I know, but what can I say? I loved the story.

An hour later, I glanced up. The house had grown quiet. The three younger boys went downstairs to watch a movie while the parents headed up to their rooms to rest. Mom asked me to make sure the twins didn't burn the house down.

Tracy slipped by after tapping me on the shoulder to tell me that she was going up to do homework. I waved to show I'd heard her, and didn't look up from the page I was on.

I glanced over at Jacob. He had his headphones in and was watching something on his phone. He'd stretched out on the couch, with his head resting on a pillow and his feet up on the other arm.

I tried to rest the book on my knees so it would look like I was reading instead of staring at him.

His dark hair fell over his forehead, and he'd occasionally brush it to the side. From this angle, I could see his long, dark lashes.

My heart picked up speed. I cleared my throat softly—worried that he would hear me—and readjusted. After trying a few different positions, I ended up with a crick in my neck. I rubbed it a few times, but there was nothing I could do except get into the hot tub and soak until I was a prune.

I closed my book and set it on the table next to me as I stood and made my way over to the stairs.

"Bailing on me, Ava?"

Jacob's teasing voice made me jump. I turned to see that he'd lowered his phone and was studying me.

"Yes," I said, my voice hoarse. Heat rushed to my cheeks as I scolded myself for being so transparent. "I'm heading to the hot tub," I confessed, and then I pinched my lips together. He hadn't asked, so why was I sharing?

He glanced around. "There's a hot tub here?"

I shrugged. "That's what my mom said." Oh man, I hoped my mom was right about that. How stupid would I feel if I came down here in my swimsuit only to find that there actually wasn't a hot tub?

But Jacob didn't ask anything else. Instead, he brought his phone back up and said, "Cool."

Realizing that our conversation was over, I nodded and made my way upstairs.

I passed by the parents' rooms and could hear snoring coming from inside. I rolled my eyes, wondering if they had a competition to see who could fall asleep the fastest. Or snore the loudest.

When I got to my room, I found Tracy sitting on her bed. She had a textbook spread across her lap. I just nodded to her when I noticed that she had in earbuds.

I grabbed my black swimsuit from the dresser and headed to the bathroom. After I changed, I wrapped my robe around my body, grabbed a towel, and headed downstairs. I tried not to feel disappointed when I discovered that Jacob had left the living room. I glanced around but didn't find him.

He must have gone up to bed or something.

I made my way through the kitchen to the back door. I grabbed my boots and headed outside. The blast of cold air hit me like a sledgehammer. I shivered as I wrapped my arms around me and sprinted over to the covered porch.

After I slid off the hot tub's cover, I pressed start on the whirlpool and waited—hugging my robe to my body and blowing on my hands to keep them from freezing. A few moments later, the water began bubbling, and steam floated up from the top of the water.

I dipped my fingers in to make sure it was warm enough. Then I pulled off my robe and boots and set them next to the towel on a chair and got in.

The warmth enveloped me as I sunk down to my chin. I closed my eyes as the bubbles surrounded me and the jets massaged my aching muscles.

I could stay here forever.

And with how cold it was out here, I really wanted to stay in the water forever. The idea of the frigid air biting my wet skin sounded like torture.

"Is there room for one more?" Jacob's low, teasing voice asked.

I yelped as I whipped my eyes open. Jacob was standing there next to the hot tub in his swim trunks and boots. His fists were clenched at his sides, and his shoulders were hunched as tried to hang on to whatever body heat he had left.

"What's the matter with you?" I asked, trying to ignore how good his chest looked in the moonlight. "Get in here," I said, waving my hand toward him.

He shot me a relieved look, slipped off his boots, and got in.

Once he was sitting across from me, it finally dawned on me that we were in the hot tub together. Jacob was half-naked and sitting in the boiling water with me.

Why?

I must have been staring at him a little too long because he laughed as he sunk down until only his head was above the water.

"Don't read into this too much," he said with a grin. "You had a good idea, coming out here, and I'm just taking advantage of it." He lifted his hand out of the water and ran it through his hair.

I dropped my gaze. If I couldn't stop staring at him before, his semi-wet hair and glistening skin wasn't going to help.

Suddenly, I felt his hand on my arm. I glanced up, startled.

He had a concerned look in his eye. "Hey, I was just joking." He glanced toward the kitchen. "I can go back inside if you don't want me here."

I shook my head. "It's a free country. Besides, there's plenty of room." I shrugged as I shot him what I hoped was a relaxed smile.

He studied me and then leaned back against the side. "That's mighty kind of you," he said in a cowboy accent as he tipped a pretend cowboy hat.

I chuckled as I leaned back and folded my arms. Was that something people did when they were relaxed? Maybe. I wasn't sure. But I was certain that I couldn't let Jacob know the effect his presence had on me.

If he found out that I was so flustered around him, he'd never let me live it down. Or he'd distance himself from me because he didn't want to lead me on. Either way, I had to keep my feelings hidden.

I could do that. Right?

CHAPTER SIX

After a few minutes of soaking in the hot tub, Jacob turned his attention over to me. I smiled and then stopped, worried I'd creep him out. When I was pretty sure I was going to die from the silence that filled the air, I moved to speak, just to have him beat me to it.

"So, how was your semester without me around?" he asked as he winked at me.

Even though I was in water that was only a few measly degrees below boiling, my cheeks heated from his question.

"I, um"—I cleared my throat—"Good."

He raised his eyebrows as he reached out and rested his arms on the edge of the tub. "Are you telling me you didn't miss me at all? Not even the tiniest bit?"

I scoffed as I dropped my gaze. I was worried that he would be able to tell that I was lying. "I honestly didn't even notice. I was like, Jacob? Who's Jacob?"

He chuckled. "Yeah. I'm sure that was how you were."

I shrugged as I moved my hands around in the water. For some reason, my nervousness manifested as fidgeting. I hoped he wouldn't think I was as much of a dork as he remembered.

"So, do you have a boyfriend?"

His question was so straightforward and unexpected that my gaze whipped up to meet his. Before I could come up with something cool like "yeah. I'm beating them off with a stick," I blurted out, "Yeah, right."

After I realized what I said, I winced and pinched my lips together.

When I looked at him again, he was watching me with intrigue.

"Really, Ava?" He ran his hands through his hair again, making it stand up on end. "I find that hard to believe."

Now my heart was galloping. "Why?"

Man, I really needed to expand my vocabulary.

He eyed me, and I literally held my breath. If he didn't start talking soon, I was going to pass out and drown in this hot tub. Granted, I would die happy, but living still seemed preferable.

"Come on, Ava. You're not that naive."

I tilted my head. How did not having a boyfriend make me naive? I knew I wasn't the hottest girl in the school. I wasn't even in the top 50%. Did he want me to admit that? I was pretty sure that the resident hottie and bad boy of our school knew that I was a nobody.

I wasn't naive—I was realistic. And it made me a tad mad that he thought I was just some junior who knew nothing about life or relationships. Sure, I'd never been kissed and never even gotten close to having a boyfriend. But I'd seen enough high school relationships to know that they weren't exactly something I needed in my life.

"I'm not naive," I said, hoping my voice would come out stronger than I felt. It didn't.

He scoffed and shook his head. "You're right, you should probably stay away from guys. It's for the best."

Now I really didn't know what he was talking about. How had

this conversation tanked so fast? And why was he talking to me this way? It was so...*older brother* of him.

Frustration flushed my body when I realized that was exactly how he saw me. I was just the little sister to his one-time best friend. Was he ever going to see me as something more? A girlfriend, perhaps?

Ugh. What was the matter with me?

I moved toward the edge of the hot tub. "I'm getting hot. I think that's my cue to get out."

When I glanced back at him, I saw him studying me. But there was something different about his gaze this time. It was like he was trying to figure out what he'd said to make me upset.

Which was totally ridiculous. He'd just basically told me that I was a kid and would always be one.

"Did I say something?" he asked.

I pinched my lips together, worried that how I really felt would slip out. "Nope." I stood, hating the fact that my swimsuit clung to my body as I climbed out.

Not wanting to see if Jacob was watching me, I wrapped my arms around my body and stepped onto the freezing ground. Thankful for my towel and robe, I slipped both on along with my shoes.

I waved at Jacob—just so he knew we were still friends, which maybe we were? Or not, I wasn't sure. Then I made my way into the house.

The movie was still on in the basement, but when I walked by the open door, I didn't hear the roughhousing that followed my brothers everywhere. They must have fallen asleep along with the rest of the house. It was eerily quiet as I walked through the rooms. The only light came from the glow of the twinkle lights that must be on a timer because they'd come on all by themselves.

I went upstairs and tried to be as quiet as I could. Tracy was asleep with her textbook in her lap and her phone in her hand. I grabbed my pajamas and slipped into the bathroom, where I pulled off my wet swimsuit and hung it on one of the towel bars.

After I rinsed off in the shower, I felt warm and comfortable as I slipped on my pajamas and pulled my damp hair into a braid at the base of my neck.

Just as I moved to climb into bed, my stomach growled.

Ugh. I was hungry. There was no way I was going to be able to sleep until I had a snack.

I padded back down the stairs and into the kitchen, where I located the hot chocolate packets and holiday cookies that I was hoping no one was saving for something special.

Just as I was pouring the hot water into a mug, the back door opened and Jacob came walking in. He, of course, had no towel. Instead, he was dripping water everywhere as he stood there like a Greek god, water droplets glistening off his toned chest.

A searing pain raced across my hand, and before I realized what was happening, I yelped and dropped the mug. The cup clattered to the counter, boiling-hot water spilling everywhere.

I waved my hand in a futile effort to dull the pain as I rushed over to the sink.

Suddenly, a warm body was standing next to me, holding my wrist. It was…Jacob.

I stared at him as he flipped on the cold water and gingerly stuck my hand under it. I winced and sucked in my breath. He turned to me with an apologetic look on his face.

"Sorry," he whispered.

I mean, that's how close we were. All he had to do was whisper, and I could hear him, even over the water. If he leaned forward, it wouldn't take that much effort to kiss me. I couldn't help but let my gaze wander down to his perfectly formed lips.

Knowing that he wanted me to respond, I just shrugged. "It's okay." I breathed out.

He pulled my hand from the water and inspected it. The skin was pink and throbbing, but thankfully, there were no blisters.

RULE #4 YOU CAN'T MISINTERPRET A MISTLETOE KISS | 43

His hand ran down my arm as he guided my fingers back under the water.

"I think you'll survive," he said.

I just nodded, hoping he couldn't hear or feel just how hard my heart was pounding.

We stood next to the sink for a few more minutes before Jacob led me over to the stove and pulled off the towel hanging from the bar and wrapped it around my hand.

I couldn't help but notice how careful he was. His fingertips were so smooth as he ran his hand across my skin that I shivered. Why did being touched feel this good? It must be because of the burn. My nerves were going haywire. In his one touch, I'd already forgotten everything that had happened in the hot tub earlier.

It also didn't help that he was so close to me that my elbow kept grazing his chest. There were a few times that I almost apologized, but I stopped myself. I didn't want to have to stop touching him if he didn't notice.

He motioned toward the table and, after he pulled out a chair for me, I sat. He took a step back and studied me.

"What were you trying to do?" he asked.

"Make myself hot chocolate."

He glanced over to the counter and then nodded. "Ah. Well, I'm going to go upstairs and get dressed. Wait for me until I come back down." He took a few steps toward the living room. "Don't touch anything until I get back."

I felt so lightheaded from the fact that he was being so caring toward me that all I could do was nod. I wasn't sure how long he was gone, but when he appeared in the doorway in a white t-shirt and flannel pajama bottoms, my heart sang. Literally.

I tried not to stare at him as he moved around the kitchen, but I couldn't help it. He was my knight in shining armor right now—as corny as that was.

After two mugs were filled with chocolatey goodness and the

cookies opened, he sat down next to me. We dunked cookies in silence.

Once I was pretty sure my stomach would burst from hot chocolate and cookies, I leaned back and shifted the towel that was still wrapped around my hand. My skin was pink but feeling better.

When I glanced up, I saw Jacob watching me. I gave him a small smile, but that didn't seem to appease him. His eyebrows were knit together.

"You okay?" he asked.

I nodded. "I'll survive."

And then a question grew in my mind. It was personal, and I worried that if I asked it, Jacob's relaxed demeanor around me would harden. Right now, I was the only one at the cabin who he was talking to. When anyone else came into the room, he shut down.

But I had to know. And the answers he'd given me in the past weren't good enough. If the Jacob he'd showed me tonight was the real Jacob, I couldn't imagine him robbing a gas station. There had to be more to this story than he was letting on.

So I let out my breath slowly and parted my lips. "Why did you do it?"

He raised his gaze to meet mine. "Do what?"

I furrowed my brow. "You know. Rob that gas station."

He scoffed and leaned back. "You still don't get it do you? You think I did it?"

I stared at him. What did that mean? "Yeah. Isn't that what the judge concluded?"

He grew quiet, and I worried that I had said something wrong. I wanted to backpedal. Go back to how it had been earlier.

He sighed. "I don't really know. Isn't that what guys like me do?"

That was his answer? He didn't know? I pushed some crumbs around on the table. "Seriously, Jacob?" I was frustrated. Heat

RULE #4 YOU CAN'T MISINTERPRET A MISTLETOE KISS | 45

pricked at the back of my neck. What was with this whole bad boy vibe he was letting off? The more I got to know Jacob the more I realized that everything he did was just a shell. A protective layer to keep those around him from knowing the real him. Was that why Andrew was so mad at him?

What was Jacob trying to prove? It was ridiculous. I'd only been around him for a day, and even I could see it was all an act.

"Why don't you act like you care about anything? Maybe if you did, your parents would respect you more." I folded my arms and studied him, wondering what he was going to say. Had I pushed it too far?

Maybe.

But it seemed as if he needed it. A normal person doesn't just go out and do whatever they wanted. There were rules, and Jacob needed to care about them. At least, he needed someone to tell him that it was important for him to care.

A smile played on his lips as he leaned forward and grabbed another cookie from the tin. He shoved it into his mouth. "Wow, Ava. I didn't know you cared that much." He quirked an eyebrow, and I could see that my reaction was amusing him.

"Is that a bad thing?" I winced. What was I doing? Why was I admitting that I cared about him? This was not how this evening was supposed to go at all.

I pushed out my chair and stood. I needed to get out of here.

His hand wrapped around my non-injured hand, halting me where I stood. I turned to see Jacob studying me.

"I'm sorry if I upset you, there's just more to the story than a simple *this is why I did it* answer," he said. His voice was low this time. There were no sly smiles or bravado. He looked—worried.

"I don't understand. Why isn't it that simple? What aren't you telling me?" I waited for a moment, but when he didn't answer, I shrugged. I was suddenly feeling very stupid with how this entire conversation had gone. I wanted to march upstairs, crawl into bed, and sleep off all of these confusing and conflicting feelings that were racing through me.

I needed some space from Jacob Stephenson. I wanted so desperately for him to trust me enough to tell me the truth, but it seemed like that was never going to happen.

Jacob was untouchable no matter how much I wanted to reach him.

"It just is," he said. "That's all I can say." His voice had dropped so low that it was almost impossible to hear him. "I'm sorry, Ava."

I swallowed, pushing all my emotions down, and said, "I'll survive." I gave him what I could only guess was a lame attempt at a smile.

He furrowed his brow for a moment before releasing my hand and turning back to his hot chocolate. "Good night, Ava." His voice sent shivers down my spine.

"Good night, Jacob," I said as I turned and hightailed it out of the room.

Once I was upstairs in the security of my bedroom, I shut the door quietly behind me and let out the breath that I'd been holding. Suddenly, my body felt like deadweight. If my goal had been to stop liking Jacob, I was failing miserably at it.

I grabbed my wrist and flexed the hand that he'd held just moments ago. I could still feel his warm fingers wrapped around mine. The caring way he looked at me as he helped with my burn. One thing was for sure, the Jacob I thought I knew was rapidly becoming a different person all together.

What was I going to do?

CHAPTER SEVEN

I woke up to yelling and the clanging of dishes. I rolled to my side to see that Tracy wasn't that thoughtful of a roommate. Instead of making sure the door was shut, she had left the light on and the door wide open.

Knowing that there was no way I was going to be able to go back to sleep, I grumbled under my breath as I got up to go to the bathroom and brush my teeth. Back in my room, I shut the door and dressed in a pair of jeans and a red turtleneck sweater. As I pulled my hair from its braid, I ran my fingers through the waves, hoping I didn't ruin the curls, and headed back into the hall.

Of course, fate's cruel sense of humor thought that was the perfect time for Jacob to come out as well. His hair was damp, and he looked amazing. He was pulling his door shut behind him, and I contemplated running back into my room. But when his gaze met mine, I froze. I didn't want him to think that I had been affected by our conversation last night, so I just gave him a smile.

"Hey," I said.

He smiled back. But I could see that he was uncomfortable. "Sleep good?" he asked.

I nodded. "Yep."

He ran his hands through his hair and then waved toward the stairs. "Breakfast?"

"Yep."

He stared at me for a moment and then started down the stairs.

Once he was at the bottom, I let out the breath I'd been holding. This was going to be such an awkward vacation if this was how we were going to act around each other. I needed to get a grip. Get over my ridiculous feelings for Jacob and move on. If I didn't, I wasn't sure I was going to last the day.

When I got to the bottom of the stairs, I saw people moving around the kitchen. Mom and Mrs. Stephenson were making breakfast. I could smell the pancakes and bacon from where I stood.

My stomach growled as I made my way into the room, sidestepping Aiden and Max who were wrestling at the opening. Jacob was standing just outside of the kitchen as if he wasn't sure where to go. I stopped a few inches behind him, waiting for him to move.

"Ooo, Jacob and Ava are standing under the mistletoe," Aiden yelled.

I stared down at him to see that he'd stopped wrestling and was pointing at something above my head. "What?" I asked.

He waved toward the spot above my head. "You and Jacob are under the mistletoe. Do you know what that means?" He wrapped both arms around his chest and made a kissy face.

I scoffed and glanced up just to see that...he was right. There was a mistletoe right above Jacob and I. Red hot embarrassment coursed through my veins.

When I lowered my gaze to meet Jacob's, I could see that he was struggling as well. His cheeks were flushed and he was having a hard time looking at me.

"We don't—I mean, you don't—" he stammered.

Before he could finish whatever he was struggling to get out,

RULE #4 YOU CAN'T MISINTERPRET A MISTLETOE KISS | 49

Mr. Stephenson tapped the corner of his newspaper onto the armchair I'd sat in yesterday and shook his head. "It's a Christmas rule, Son," he said.

I whipped my gaze over to him. Was he serious? He was going to make me *kiss* Jacob. Here? Now?

"I'm good," I said, raising my hand and shaking my head.

"Ah, come on. It's just a kiss." Mom piped up as she suddenly appeared next to us.

Great. My first kiss ever, and my entire family was here to witness it. Well, not only witness it, but strong-arm the guy into doing it. I could literally feel my self-esteem sink ten feet.

When I managed to bring my gaze up to meet Jacobs, I saw a hint of desperation in his eyes. Wow, the nails to my confidence's coffin were getting driven in deeper and deeper.

"I think we have to," he said, stepping toward me.

Have to. Words every girl dreams of hearing right before they kiss their lifelong crush. But, knowing there was no way I could run away, I shrugged—taking an *I don't care* page from Jacob's book.

"Fine," I said, stepping closer to him.

We stood there for only a few seconds, but they felt like a lifetime. He leaned toward me, and in a movement so fast that it left me wondering if it had really happened, he pressed his lips to mine and pulled back.

"Happy?" he asked.

I stared at him, wondering if he had really touched me. And then my heart plummeted. I was so gross to him that he couldn't even kiss me. This was horrible.

"That was the most ridiculous kiss I've ever seen," Mr. Stephenson said. "Do it again. Show her how a Stephenson kisses."

I turned to glare at Mr. Stephenson, but if he noticed, he didn't care. He just set his jaw and stared Jacob down.

"Oh, no. I think it's the other way around, Ava should show

Jacob how a Rogers kisses." Mom stepped closer to me, moving her hands together as if directing how it should be done.

And then I realized that my first kiss had become a competition. Stephenson versus Rogers. Who was going to kiss the best? This was all sorts of weird, but when our parents got an idea in their head, they weren't going to let it go.

"I'm not sure I want this to be a competition," Jacob said. His voice was quiet. He looked about as uncomfortable as I felt.

"Come on, Son. It's just a kiss," Mrs. Stephenson said as she appeared next to us.

I glanced over at Jacob, whose eyebrows knitted together and jaws flexed like he wanted to say something.

"Mom," he said under his breath.

I'd had enough of this nonsense. I was tired of trying to analyze everything Jacob was doing. I liked him and I was going to kiss him, dang it. I was going to blow his socks off in true Rogers's fashion—whatever that was.

Reaching up, I grabbed each of his cheeks and pulled his lips down to mine. Tingles erupted across my body and shot out of my toes as I held him there.

Then, as if he'd finally realized what I was doing, his hands felt their way to my sides and slid to my back as he pulled me closer.

Seconds turned to hours as we stood there, lips pressed together. I could hear hoots and hollers from the bystanders, but I didn't care. All I could think about was Jacob.

I moved my hands to thread my fingers through his hair and deepen the kiss. Our lips moved against each other as if this came as naturally as breathing. In all my daydreams of kissing Jacob, they hadn't come close to the exhilarating feeling that raced through me now.

Just when I was sure I was going to melt into a puddle, he pulled back.

"There," he said, pushing me away with his hands.

I stumbled back, watching him as he ducked his head and

RULE #4 YOU CAN'T MISINTERPRET A MISTLETOE KISS | 51

disappeared into the kitchen. I pressed my fingertips against my lips as I watched his hasty retreat. As much as I hated to admit it, my heart literally broke inside of my chest. There had been something in that kiss. Something that he had to have felt too. Why was he walking away from me? Why was he still acting like he didn't care?

Mom patted my back and told me, "That's how a Rogers does it." Weird. I moved away because I really didn't feel like celebrating with her. There was nothing joyous about kissing a guy you'd cared about for years, just to have him push you away and storm off.

Had I done something wrong?

And then I felt stupid. Of course I'd done something wrong. Didn't Jacob say I was naive? I had never kissed someone before. For all I knew, I'd bit him or something.

The crowd that had formed around us to witness our kiss dispersed, and soon I was left alone with my thoughts. Great. Just what I needed.

I wrapped my arm around my stomach and slowly moved into the kitchen. Jacob was sitting at the table with his back to me. Grateful that I would have a moment away from him to gather my thoughts, I turned to Mom, who was dishing up a plate of eggs for me.

She was talking to Mrs. Stephenson about the plan for the day.

Suddenly, Mrs. Stephenson let out a groan. "Who ate the cookies that we were going to dip in chocolate and use to decorate the gingerbread houses?" she asked, holding up the tin of cookies that Jacob and I had consumed the night before.

I moved to step forward and take responsibility, but Jacob beat me to it. He turned around and pointed to himself.

"I did," he said.

It hurt my heart how fast Mrs. Stephenson's expression changed. It went from annoyed to angry. And for some strange reason, rage coursed through me. Why was she like this with

Jacob? She had to know her own son. Sure, he'd just rejected me after our first kiss, but that didn't make him a bad guy.

And it made me so angry that his mother couldn't see that.

"Why would you do that? Didn't you learn anything about taking stuff that isn't yours?" Mrs. Stephenson dropped the tin down onto the counter and folded her arms.

Jacob just shrugged. "Sorry," he said and turned back to his food.

I stepped forward. There was no way he was going to take all the blame when it was my fault. "Actually, Mrs. Stephenson, it was me."

Mrs. Stephenson glanced over and gave me a sympathetic look. She'd been so mad at Jacob, why were her eyes wide and her forehead relaxed when she was looking at me? I'd just admitted to eating the apparently special cookies "It's okay, sweetheart. You don't have to take the blame." Then she leaned in toward me. "I understand that Jacob can seem like someone you want to protect, but he's never going to learn if we don't hold him accountable."

My mouth dropped open. Did she seriously just say that? About her own son? Sure, my parents weren't perfect, but they always gave us the benefit of the doubt. This—what Mrs. Stephenson was doing—was just mean.

"Well, you should be upset with me because I ate them as well," I said, but Mrs. Stephenson looked as if she'd already moved on. She just gave me a small smile and turned back to Jacob.

"You'll be going back into town to buy another tin of cookies," she said to the back of Jacob's head.

His shoulders tightened, and then he relaxed as he grabbed his plate of food and stood. "Fine," he said as he walked past her and dumped his dishes into the sink.

I watched, dumbfounded as he passed by me. Andrew, who must have just woke up from the way his blond hair was standing up in all directions, was standing in the doorway watching us.

Jacob didn't attempt to slip past him, instead, he rammed Andrew's shoulder and then disappeared upstairs.

I was so mad that there weren't any words that I could think to say. How could someone's own mother treat them that way?

And apparently, I was the only one who cared, because in no time at all, the normal kitchen conversations returned. Everyone was acting like nothing had happened.

I clenched my fists as I made my way toward the opening of the kitchen where Andrew still stood, looking a little flabbergasted.

Right when I passed by, Andrew grabbed my arm.

"What's going on?" he asked.

I glanced over at him, annoyed that he was getting in my way. "Mrs. Stephenson just freaked out on Jacob because we ate the tin of cookies that they were saving." I had to force my voice to remain calm—that's how angry I was.

Andrew's gaze ran over my face. "Where are you going, then?"

I stared at him. He had to see how unfairly Jacob's parents were treating him. "That wasn't cool. I'm going to make sure that I go along with Jacob." I leaned into Andrew. "I ate the cookies, but Mrs. Stephenson didn't care. She told me to stop defending Jacob. That 'he'll never learn' or something."

Andrew's jaw set—he seemed just as upset as I was. Good. He finally understood why I was mad.

And then words I didn't expect to hear tumbled out of his mouth. "Maybe you should just stay away from him, Ava. His mom knows best."

I took a step back, pulling my arm from Andrew's grasp. "What are you talking about?"

He shrugged as he pushed his hands through his hair. "Maybe Mrs. Stephenson knows how to handle Jacob. Maybe she's right."

I stared at him. "Mrs. Stephenson was wrong to treat Jacob that way."

Andrew's cheeks reddened as he cleared his throat. "I guess I just don't want to see you get hurt," he mumbled.

I shook my head and passed by him. I was tired of listening to him. What was with the people in this house? It was like I was living in the twilight zone.

Jacob came pounding down the stairs just as I passed by. I scrambled to catch up with him, but he was too fast. He had the front door open and closed before I could get any words out.

I grabbed my boots and coat and ran out after him.

"Jacob," I called out. Slushy snow seeped into my socks, but I didn't care.

"Leave it, Ava," he called over his shoulder. He had his keys out and was unlocking the driver's door of his parents' van.

Not listening, I raced over to the passenger door and pulled it open. He grumbled, but I didn't care. Instead, I hopped up into the seat and shut the door.

Determination rushed through me as I stared him down. He just looked at me with his brow furrowed, pain written across his face.

"What are you doing?" he asked.

I tightened my seatbelt. "I'm coming with you."

He paused and then sighed. "Fine."

CHAPTER EIGHT

Heat blasted from the vents as Jacob drove down the street, heading toward the highway that would take us to the grocery store. Tall evergreen trees whipped past us. The sun shone down on their snow-sprinkled tips. Any other time, I would have remarked on its beauty, but Jacob didn't seem in the mood, so I kept my lips clamped shut.

Instead, I focused on peeling off my sopping-wet socks. I rolled them into a ball and set them on the floor next to me.

"Why did you do that?" Jacob asked. His voice was emotionally charged and made me shiver.

I glanced over at him, and he nodded toward my socks. "Why did I run out after you without any shoes?" I asked.

A smile tugged at his lips. "Yeah."

I shrugged. "You weren't stopping for anyone. What was I supposed to do?" I slipped on my boots, wiggling my toes in the soft, sherpa lining. It wasn't ideal, but at least I'd be warm.

"You could try not following me," he whispered.

A little taken back by his reaction, I studied him. "Your mom was wrong," I said. I wanted him to know that even though everyone else in the room had seemed okay with what happened, I wasn't.

He glanced over at me and held my gaze. Every part of me tingled from the intensity in his eyes. Then he shrugged and turned back to the road.

"That's where you're wrong, Ava," he said, clutching the steering wheel so hard that his knuckles turned white.

"I'm not wrong," I said, and then a moment later, I whispered, "and I'm not naive."

When he didn't respond, I peeked over at him. He was staring a bit too hard at the road. Like he was fighting an internal battle. Was it wrong that I wanted him to open up to me? To finally show me the true Jacob?

I was tired of him not responding, so I decided to take the conversation in a different direction. "Why did you say you ate the cookies when it was the two of us?"

He shrugged. "I'm a delinquent. People expect it from me. I'm used to taking the blowback."

I stared at him. That was a strange reaction. "What else have you taken the blowback from?"

He cleared his throat and shifted in his seat. "It doesn't matter. It's in the past." He glanced over at me with pleading in his eyes. "Can we just move on?"

I folded my arms. I wasn't happy with that answer, but the look in his eyes told me to let it go, so I sighed and nodded. "Sure. If you promise you'll tell me in the future."

A smiled twitched on his lips. "We have a future?"

Heat burned my cheeks when I realized what he meant. I cleared my throat and nodded. "Sure. Yeah. Whatever."

Jacob wrapped his fingers around mine and squeezed. "Thanks for standing up for me, Ava."

My head lightened as I swallowed and glanced over at him. Did he feel the heat that radiated between the two of us? Or was it just me? Oh man, how I prayed that he felt it too.

"Of course. It was the right thing to do," I said, hating that my voice was so breathy.

He shrugged as he pulled his hand back and returned it to the steering wheel. My hand felt cold in the absence of his touch. I threaded my fingers together in my lap.

"Well, that's a trait that doesn't seem to run through everyone," he mumbled.

I turned to study him. Did he mean someone specific or in general? And then I felt stupid. Of course, he was talking about his mom. Doing the right thing seemed to definitely be lacking in her.

"It's okay. I'm sure she'll come around." I smiled. A mom couldn't hate her son forever. At some point, Mrs. Stephenson was going to realize that she was wrong and fix the broken relationship between them.

We were stopped at a red light, and Jacob stared at me like I had two heads. " 'She,' meaning your mom."

The car behind us honked, and Jacob whipped his gaze up to the rearview mirror.

"It's green," I said, waving to the light in front of us.

He pressed on the gas and waved to the other driver. After a minute, he relaxed.

Silence fell around us, and I wasn't sure if I was supposed to keep talking or if it was his turn to talk,

Five minutes later, we pulled into Food 'n Save, and Jacob turned off the car. He pulled the keys from the ignition and grabbed his wallet and phone from the center console. He stared at his screen, and after a few seconds, he sighed. "My mom wants us to pick up powdered sugar, food dye, and molasses."

I nodded as I pulled on the door handle and stepped out, committing the list to memory. "Got it," I said.

When we got into the grocery store, I grabbed a cart, and Jacob followed after me as the front doors slid open and we walked into the produce section.

After a few seconds of wandering around, I realized that Jacob didn't know where to find the things we needed. I smiled as I nodded at him. "Follow me," I said.

Relief flooded Jacob's face as I lead him over to the baking aisle.

"I'll grab the molasses, and you get the sugar," I said over my shoulder as I rolled the cart to the glass jars that lined the far end of the aisle, not waiting for his reply. I mean, it was powdered sugar, not rocket science.

Once I'd grabbed a few jars—just to be safe—I turned to see Jacob walking up behind me. He had a five-pound bag of granulated sugar in his hands. He smiled as he set it down into the cart.

I stared at him. "That's the wrong sugar."

He glanced down. "It's sugar."

I laughed. "Yeah, but it's granulated. The stuff we are looking for is *powdered*," I said, dragging out each syllable.

He stared at me. "What's the difference?" He shuffled closer to me. Like, centimeters from me.

My senses went into hyperdrive. Was he going to kiss me again? It seemed strange, but if he wanted to, I was game. Plus, I wanted to see what it would be like to kiss him without the audience we had earlier.

He reached his arm out, and I couldn't help it, I leaned in closer to him. I wanted to feel his arms around me again, pulling me closer to him.

"Like this?" he asked, pulling a bag of powdered sugar off the shelf next to me.

Instantly, I felt like an idiot. As if I'd been hit with a jolt of lightening, I jumped away from him. My heart was hammering so hard, and I felt like a complete idiot.

Inside, I was praising myself for not going up on my tiptoes and kissing him. That would have been a colossal mistake.

When I finally settled down, I glanced over at Jacob. He held the bag of sugar in his hands like he didn't know what he was supposed to do with it.

"Yes," I whispered and then cleared my throat. "I mean, yes. That's the right sugar." I forced a smile. "Good job."

He nodded as he placed the bag into the cart. Then he grabbed the granulated sugar and returned it to the shelf. When he turned back, he gave me a small smile. "Food dye?"

I nodded and moved down the aisle to where the frosting was located. After grabbing a box, we headed toward the cookie aisle to get a container to replace the ones we'd eaten. Thankfully, there weren't any more almost-kisses by the time we checked out.

We stayed pretty far away from each other as we walked across the parking lot and dumped the bags into the trunk. Once we were inside of the car and Jacob started the engine, I began to relax. This wasn't so bad. I could survive being around Jacob for the rest of our time here if I just stayed a safe distance away from him.

Far enough to breathe, but not so far that he'd think I was being aloof.

When we got back to the cabin, everyone seemed to have been hard at work. The two Christmas trees were fully decorated and filmed—according to Mom. We were practically attacked when we walked into the kitchen. Apparently, they needed the molasses to start the gingerbread houses.

Jacob and I willingly released our hold on the bags and stepped to the outskirts of the kitchen while flour was measured and mixing bowls started up.

I glanced over at Jacob, who was studying me. Heat flushed my cheeks under his stare, but somehow I mustered the strength to hold his gaze and even send him a smile.

He narrowed his eyes and then turned and headed toward the basement, calling out to anyone who was listening that he was going to watch a Christmas movie. Even though I wanted to join him, I stayed rooted to my spot. Eventually Mrs. Stephenson took notice and demanded that I help or get out of the way.

Taking that as my cue to grab an apron and dig in, I let myself get swallowed up in the holiday baking storm that was raging around me. At least, with something to do, I wouldn't have time to focus on Jacob and all of the feelings that came over me when I thought about him.

Hopefully I would be away from him for long enough to get the wall built up around my heart that I'd been trying hard to construct ever since we got here. Maybe once it was up, I'd be able to survive this holiday season.

CHAPTER NINE

The gingerbread house pieces were out of the oven and resting on cooling racks when Jacob finally came back upstairs. He was carrying Max over his shoulder. Max was squealing and wiggling, stating that this was not the way you played cops and robbers and he was going to report Jacob to the authorities.

Jacob just laughed, lowered his brother down, and ruffled Max's hair.

I tried not to stare as I shifted uncomfortably on the kitchen chair that I had been forced to sit on. After I burned a few batches, Mrs. Stephenson banished me from touching the food and set me on cookie-watching duty. Apparently, if anyone came in and tried to steal a gingerbread piece, I was to swat their hand away.

Max protested to Jacob's show of affection. He slipped away from Jacob and sprinted to the basement door, slamming it behind him.

Now alone, I tried to look inconspicuous as I focused on the book in front of me. I wasn't sure what I wanted to happen. Did I want Jacob to talk to me or just leave me alone?

The chair beside me scraped against the floor. And the butterflies in my stomach answered my question. Jacob was going to hang out with me. I forced myself to relax.

When I saw Jacob reach out to grab a bit of the gingerbread, instinct kicked in, and I reached up and swatted his hand. He laughed as he pulled it back.

"What was that for?" he asked.

I shrugged as I folded the corner of the page I'd been reading and turned to look at him. "Just following your mom's directions."

He crossed his arms over his chest and studied me. "My mom told you to hurt people?"

I nodded. "Something like that."

He shook his head. "That doesn't seem like her," he said with sarcasm coating his words.

I fiddled with the jacket cover of the book. I wasn't sure where to go next. We'd spent a lot of our time together here. In these back-and-forth, flirty conversations.

Every time I tried to bring up something deeper, he'd either shut me down or change the subject.

Before I could speak, Andrew walked in. His gaze landed on me and Jacob, and I saw his expression tighten. I half-expected him to leave from the way he was glaring at Jacob, and I about fell out of my chair when he took the seat next to me.

I gave him a smile. Besides our conversation earlier, Andrew and I hadn't really talked at all today. Despite his feelings about Jacob, I wasn't going to turn my back on my brother. He was family, after all.

"Whatcha doing?" I asked.

He shrugged. "Trying to find something to do."

I snorted. "So you came down here? All I'm doing is watching these cookies so Mrs. Stephenson doesn't have my head if they get stolen."

"Oh, you mean these—" He started to reach out, and with catlike reflexes, I swatted his hand away.

He shook his hand in mock pain. "Geez. So much for being family."

I shrugged. "I value my life over your stomach."

Andrew chuckled, and then the air fell silent.

"Why don't we play a card game?" I asked. I hated sitting here in silence, feeling the tension emanating off of both of them. I'd be Switzerland if I had to be. Besides, wasn't it time that they got over the past? And if they weren't ready, I sure as heck was.

"I'm not sure," Jacob said. I could feel him twitching uncomfortably next to me. I wanted to reach out and rest my hand on his so he'd calm down. His agitation was making me nervous but I refrained, convincing myself that touching him would freak him out more than calm him down.

I glanced over at him and smiled. "It'll be fun. Come on, let's go see what games they have."

Jacob studied me and then sighed. "Fine. I'll play."

I clapped my hands and pushed out my chair. "Yes, this is going to be so fun."

But before Jacob moved, Andrew stood. "I'll help you. You can wait here, Jacob."

I stared at my brother. That seemed a bit rude. I moved to say something, but Jacob just shrugged.

"Better for me," he said as he settled back into his chair.

Andrew and I walked into the living room together. I tried to keep my frustration about what he'd said pushed down. Why was he acting like this? I knew that Jacob had hurt him, but it was time to move on.

"That was rude," I said, glancing over and giving him my signature *I'm annoyed with you* look.

Andrew brushed it off as he pulled open the cabinets that ran along the far wall. "I'm not sure what you are talking about."

I scoffed. "Seriously? You are being really mean to Jacob."

Andrew stopped moving and turned to look at me. "Wait, are you defending him?" He narrowed his eyes. "Why? What did he tell you?" He shook his head. "I knew he was just spending time with you to get to me."

I wasn't sure what the heck he was talking about, and frustration built up inside of me. Was I just a pawn to the two of them? I hadn't thought of that before. Were they just using me to get back at each other? Is that why Jacob had been so nice to me?

Bile rose up in my throat, but I muscled it back down. That was ridiculous. First, I was giving way too much credit to the boys who used to put glue in their hair and ate mud growing up. Second, I didn't want to think that the only reason Jacob would spend time with me was to get back at my brother.

But, the more I let that thought linger in my mind, the more real it became. Could it be true? No. I was just being stupid. Right?

Frustrated and angry, I glared at Andrew as I grabbed *Sorry*. "I have no idea what you are talking about, but I'm tired of the way you two are acting. You're acting like children, and I'm not getting in the middle of it anymore." I hugged the game to my chest and raised my chin defiantly. "Now, put aside whatever it is between you and let's play a game."

Andrew watched me for a second before he sighed. "Fine."

Thankful that he wasn't going to argue with me, I led him back into the kitchen where Jacob was still sitting at the table.

After we set up the game, we started to play. A few rounds into it, I could feel the tension slowly start to dissipate. I even allowed myself to wonder if, perhaps, we'd finally reached a point where they no longer hated each other.

And then Andrew knocked Jacob's piece off the board. Literally. It sailed across the kitchen and plopped into the sink with a small *tink*.

Jacob glared at him. Andrew, of course, had a triumphant grin on his face as he sat back in his chair.

The tension was not only back, but it had increased four hundred percent.

RULE #4 YOU CAN'T MISINTERPRET A MISTLETOE KISS | 65

"It's just a game, *Jake*," Andrew said.

I winced at his mocking tone. I glared at Andrew, but he didn't seem to notice. He was too busy smirking. It made me really want to punch him.

Jacob shrugged. "Don't get too cocky. I may have taken the fall last time, but next time, it's on you." He held Andrew's gaze as he folded his arms and leaned back.

From the corner of my eye, I saw Andrew's smile fade. I furrowed my brow, suddenly getting the feeling that they were talking about something very different than this game of Sorry.

"I didn't ask for your pawn to be there," Andrew said, his tone growing more strained by the minute.

Jacob scoffed. "Typical. It's my fault for getting in your way." Jacob pushed his hands through his hair. "I should have known that was the kind of friend you'd turn out to be. Nice true colors."

I was tired of this weird conversation, so I raised my hand, hoping it would silence the two of them. It didn't.

Andrew leaned forward. "You're not the saint you try to paint yourself as. You didn't have to take the fall. You could have spoken up." Andrew's face was red now, contrasting against his blond hair.

What the heck was he talking about? "Andrew—" I started, but Jacob cut me off.

"I never said I was a saint. I'm just a good friend. I'm sorry if you don't know what that is. 'Cause for as long as I can remember, you've been a pretty crappy one." Jacob pushed his chair back, the legs scraping against the floor. "I'm done playing," he said as his pained and frustrated gaze met mine.

I couldn't stop him. Before I'd opened my lips, he was across the kitchen and disappearing into the living room. Frustrated with the way this entire evening had gone down, I turned to glare at Andrew.

He shrugged his shoulders. "What?" he asked as he flicked a

few game pieces off the table. They clinked as they landed on the floor.

I punched his arm, and he winced but didn't move.

"What are you talking about, 'what'? What is the matter with you? Why are you treating Jacob like that?" I was so frustrated with my brother that it was choking my throat. I wanted them to get along—no needed them to. I was pretty sure I had a better chance of getting those two to be friends again than I did of forcing myself to stop liking Jacob.

"You guys used to be friends. I'm sure you could figure out how to do it again." Man, even I could hear the desperation in my voice.

Andrew shook his head as he pushed away from the table. "You don't understand, Ava. You never will. Stop trying to get us to be friends again. It's over." He held up his hand as he turned away from me. "Just leave me alone."

I watched as my brother walked out of the room and disappeared downstairs. Now alone, I slouched in my chair. Tears pricked my eyes. What was I going to do? Both Jacob and Andrew seemed ticked off at me, and I wasn't sure how to fix any of this. Sure, both of them had continually told me that no matter what I said or did, I couldn't change things between them. But there was something deep down in my gut that told me to keep trying.

Since Andrew told me to my face to leave him alone, I decided to try my mediation skills on Jacob. After all, I didn't want to let that one class I took last year go to waste.

So I stood and headed over to the stairs. I took them two at a time, and before I really had time to prepare my opening argument in my mind, I was standing in front of Jacob's door with my hand raised, ready to knock.

But, for some reason, I couldn't bring myself to actually hit my knuckles against the wood. My insecurities about our relationship were growing. What if I'd made it all up? What if Jacob was just being nice to me?

If I ran all of the situations we'd been put in through my mind, he had either either forced by his parents or I'd forced myself on him. Except for the hot tub—he'd voluntarily gotten in there with me. But for all I knew, he'd just been really sore and needed a soak. I was just the weird, geeky girl who'd happened to be there.

Just as I dropped my hand and turned away, grateful that no one saw me standing here, the door opened and Jacob's startled gaze met mine.

"Wh—what are you doing here?" Jacob asked, letting go of the door and folding his arms.

I shrugged. "I'm apologizing?"

He studied me for a moment and then sighed. "Did Andrew send you?"

I shook my head. "No. I wanted to let you know that I didn't mean to force you to speak to my brother. I know you guys have something against each other that I don't understand, and I really shouldn't have taken it upon myself to get you to fix your issues when you weren't ready." My face began to heat as his eyebrows rose and his lips tipped up into a smile.

When I finally drew breath, he chuckled.

"Are you done?"

I tipped my head forward and nodded, wishing that the floor would just open up and swallow me whole. "Yes," I whispered.

And then, he did something strange. He grabbed my elbow and pulled me into his room. And shut the door.

I stared at him. Was he bringing me in here so that he could yell at me in private? I widened my eyes as I tried not to analyze his every move. I didn't want to creep him out, and I didn't want to read too much into what he was doing, like at the grocery store.

"Geez, Ava, you look terrified," he said, pressing on my lower back and motioning toward the desk chair a few feet away.

I forced my face to relax and smiled tightly. "I do?"

He chuckled. "Yeah. It's like you've never been alone with a guy before."

My stomach twisted. Well, that was true. There weren't too many guys—none, in fact—that were lining up to sit in a room alone with Ava Rogers. That just wasn't something that happened in my universe.

Once I was sitting, I found him studying me.

"You *have* been alone with a guy before, right?"

I didn't want to lie even though my head was telling me I should. I still wanted there to be a bit of mystery between Jacob and I. And I was worried if I opened my lips and confirmed what he suspected, we would lose this, whatever it was, that was happening between us.

I shook my head.

He scoffed. "I find that hard to believe." And then he stopped and stared at me. "Have you never kissed a guy? I mean, besides the mistletoe thing downstairs."

I brought my knees up so I could bury my face in them. I'm sure my cheeks were beet red by now, and even if I tried to lie, my embarrassment would give me away.

"Wow. Now I'm really surprised. I would have guessed…" His voice trailed off as if he too was suddenly extremely embarrassed.

But his comment had me interested. I had to know what he was going to say. And I wasn't leaving until he spit it out.

CHAPTER TEN

*J*acob chuckled as he moved to sit on the bed. He rested his hands on his knees as he glanced around the room. I could tell that he was trying to look anywhere but at me, and that intrigued me. Suddenly, I wasn't the only one who was struggling to figure out where we stood.

He was nervous.

I straightened, using my new-found discovery to fuel my confidence. If he was nervous, that had to mean something. I just had to get that something out of him without revealing how I felt about him. Because if I was wrong, I was in trouble.

"What were you going to say?" I asked at the same time he asked "What are you doing here?"

We both pinched our lips together and studied each other.

Finally, he sighed and ran his hands through his hair. "Why did you come in here, Ava? I think the interaction between me and your brother spoke for itself. We're never going to be friends again. It's over."

I parted my lips. I wanted to say something. Give him a glimmer of hope. It was Christmas after all. Wasn't this supposed to be a time of healing? Of magic? But then, I realized that Jacob didn't want that. He was hurting, and the more I told him to just get over it, the worse it got.

So I shrugged and changed what I was going to say. "I know. Andrew is being a dork about this. He should be able to move on from whatever happened. I mean, after all, you two were best friends." I chewed my lip. What was I supposed to say? *If you don't get along with my brother, nothing can happen between us?*

Yeah, there was no way that was going to go over well.

When I brought my attention back to Jacob, his brows were furrowed and he was staring at me intensely. Like he was trying to figure me out or something.

I wrapped my arms around my knees and rested my chin on top of them. Did I want to show him how I felt? Did I want him to know that I couldn't help but like him?

Maybe.

He sighed and shifted until he was lying on the bed, propped up by one elbow. "You really want your brother and me to be friends again, don't you?"

I shrugged, grabbing the desk next to me and pushing myself into a spin. "What's wrong with that?"

I got a few peeks at him as I spun around. He was watching me, and that annoying smile of his was back. When I finally forced myself to stop because it was making me sick, I found that he'd moved. Instead of lying on the bed, he'd pulled up another desk chair and was seated right next to me.

He winked at me as he began spinning himself. I giggled.

"You're going to make yourself puke, like I'm about to," I said, puffing my cheeks out.

He shrugged. "It looks fun," he said as he spun himself faster and faster.

Not wanting to be bested by Jacob, I reached out and followed suit. Soon, I was spinning so fast that everything around me had become a blur. Just when I was pretty sure my brain couldn't handle the centrifugal force, I stopped the chair and rose up onto my shaking legs.

"Where are you going?" Jacob called after me.

I shook my head. I just needed to get out of that chair.

"Hey, hang on, you're super wobbly," Jacob said, appearing next to me.

I felt his hand grab my arm, but he must have been just as unstable as I was because the room spun and we were both suddenly falling to the ground.

"Jacob!" I squealed as I landed smack dab on top of him. I heard the air leave his lungs in a giant *whoosh*. I squeezed my eyes shut, praying the world would stop spinning.

After a good minute, my head felt as if it were coming back together, so I peeked out. Jacob was lying with his head back and his eyes closed. He didn't look miserable, like I felt. Instead, he looked…calm.

It wasn't until now that I realized his hands were wrapped around my upper arms. The warmth from his fingers permeated through my sweater.

My heart began to pound. I knew he could feel it. I could feel it in my toes.

"Jacob," I whispered, not sure what to think of any of this. Did he like this? Did he want me to stay?

He lifted his head and squinted at me. "You okay?" he asked. His voice had dropped to a low rumble. I tried not to read into that as I nodded.

"I think so."

He smiled, leaned his head back, and closed his eyes. But he didn't move away from me. His hands were still on my arms, and our bodies were touching, and he seemed perfectly okay with that.

How could I not read into that? Did he like me being close?

I should really get up.

"I think I'm going to be okay now," I said. My voice was barely above a whisper. I think it was partly because I didn't want him to let me go, and partly because I was nervous to give my mouth free reign. There were way too many thoughts rolling around in my mind, and I needed to leave before I spoke any of them.

In one swift movement, Jacob rolled me off his chest and then propped himself up right next to me with his arm draped over my stomach. Now, I was sandwiched between him and the floor.

"Ava," he said, reaching up and brushing my hair away from my face.

My heart was pounding so hard, I couldn't breathe. Or maybe it was because the weight of his arm was cutting my lung capacity in half. I didn't care. I didn't want him to go anywhere.

I met his gaze and responded, "Jacob."

He smiled, and I could see his flirty side emerge. "Have you really never kissed anyone before?"

I broke our gaze to stare up at the ceiling. I forced a contemplative expression, hoping I came across as thoughtful—and perhaps teasing as well? If only I were that smooth.

I sucked my breath through my teeth and shook my head. "I don't believe I ever said that."

He studied me when I brought my gaze back to him. "Yeah, I think you said you've never been alone with a guy."

I chuckled and shrugged. "It's because I like to make out with guys when my parents are watching to give me pointers." I waved my hand between his chest and mine. "Case in point."

His brow furrowed, and then he smiled. "Should we go downstairs, then?"

Whoa. Where was this conversation going? "Why?" I whispered, my confidence deflating.

"Because I'd like to kiss you again."

I swallowed. "Really?"

He leaned closer. I became very aware of every point of contact between us. His leg was pressed against mine. His arm

RULE #4 YOU CAN'T MISINTERPRET A MISTLETOE KISS | 73

was warm againt my sweater. His chest—his hard and well-defined chest—was pressed against mine.

And then there were his lips. They were perfectly shaped and were coming very close to my own.

"Are you sure?" I asked as I tipped my face up to his.

He hesitated, meeting my gaze.

"I mean, if you decide you don't want to, I totally understand. After all, sometimes I say things that I don't mean, and I always wish I could take them back." I really needed to stop talking.

He chuckled as he leaned forward and brushed his lips against mine. It was such a soft and gentle movement, but my whole body responded. My heart pounded and my lips tingled. I even closed my eyes so I could memorize the feeling of his lips meeting mine.

"Ava," he said.

I tipped my face closer to his but didn't open my eyes. "Um hmm," I responded.

"You talk too much."

Just as I began to protest, Jacob leaned forward and pressed his lips to mine. With that one movement, all I could think about was how right all of this felt.

How right Jacob felt.

The guy that I had crushed on for so long was kissing me. Me! And there weren't any parents around to pressure him into doing it.

Excitement coursed through my veins as I lifted my hands and ran them through his hair. He responded by pressing closer to me. I was pretty sure he was crushing my lungs, but I didn't care. I'd rather pass out than have him stop kissing me.

He pulled back, and I tried not to groan. I glanced up at him. My gaze was hazy and my lips felt puffy. Why had he stopped? Did I do something wrong?

"Ava," he said.

I studied him. "Yeah?"

"I like you."

My ears were ringing. Like, I was pretty sure he'd just said that he liked me, but I wasn't sure. Just in case I misheard him, I asked, "Really?"

He reached up and fiddled with my hair. "Yeah. I do." His gaze returned to mine. "Do you... How do you feel about me?"

Oh. Right. I was supposed to respond. I squeezed my eyes shut for a moment, gathering my courage. "Promise not to think I'm a dork?"

He chuckled. I loved the fact that I could feel it against my chest. "Sure."

I refused to open my eyes as I confessed my crush. "I've liked you for...a long time." I peeked under my lids, hoping to gauge his reaction. He looked amused.

"I knew it."

I whipped my eyes open and shoved his shoulder, which barely moved him. He laughed and dropped his chest back so he was next to me again.

"You did not." I protested.

He shrugged. "I can read you like a book, Rogers."

I rolled my eyes. "Yeah, well..." Wow. That was my response? It must be his kisses. They were my brain's kryptonite.

He leaned closer and pressed his lips against my forehead. "I like that you're open," he said as he pulled back and studied me.

Finding confidence that I didn't know I had, I reached up and pulled him down, crushing my lips against his.

This time, I didn't think. I just felt. I wanted to know everything there was to know about Jacob Stephenson. He'd been such a mystery to me, and finally, he was opening up.

Jacob deepened the kiss. Everything felt perfect. Everything felt right.

That should have been the first signal to me that something was about to go wrong.

"What is going on in here?" Mrs. Stephenson's voice cut through the air like a hot knife.

I froze. My body instantly went numb.

"What are you doing to her?" she asked, her voice coming out shrill.

I winced and sprang away from Jacob. My gaze made its way to the doorway, where I saw Mom and Mrs. Stephenson standing there, slack-jawed.

"Ava," Mom breathed. She had her hand pressed to her chest as she stared at me. "Are you okay?"

Mrs. Stephenson scoffed as she took a few steps into the room. "I'm so sorry." She shot Mom a sympathetic expression. "Jacob... I..." Mrs. Stephenson swallowed. "We should have known better than to bring him here." She held up her hands. "I didn't..."

I scrambled to my feet. "It's not what it looks like. We were spinning in the chairs and fell down. Then we..." How was I supposed to explain the fact that we were just kissing? That we both just happened to land perfectly on the other person's mouth?

Mrs. Stephenson stepped closer to me. She had her arms out and began ushering me away from Jacob. "Come here, sweetheart. We know it's not your fault." She shoved me toward my mom and then turned her attention toward Jacob.

Jacob looked stunned as he stared at his mom. "I wasn't...I mean, that's not what happened." He ran his hands through his hair, and I could see the pain written across his face. He was hurting.

And I was just standing here, doing nothing.

"I kissed him," I said, stepping forward and ignoring the fact that Mom was trying to pull me back.

Jacob held up his hand to silence me. "It's no use," he said under his breath before turning to face Mrs. Stephenson. "You're right, Mom. I am a bad influence. You should have never brought me here." He stepped forward. "I'm sorry, Ava," he said, tipping his face toward me without looking at me.

I was flabbergasted. It was one thing to take the blame for eating some cookies. But taking the blame for our kiss was just so...*frustrating*. It made me so mad that every rational thought flew from my mind. All I could think about was the fact that he was negating everything he'd just said to me.

A guy who liked me would stand up to his parents. He would fight for me—for us. He wouldn't just walk away. He wouldn't let his mom say things about him—about us—that weren't true. And if he wasn't going to do any of those things, then I was. I wasn't chicken.

"Mrs. Stephenson!" I finally blurted out. As I stood there, my brain literally screeched to a halt.

Everyone was staring at me, expecting me to continue. And I wanted to. Oh, how I wanted to. But nothing, no rational argument, would form in my brain.

Mrs. Stephenson's expression morphed into one of understanding. "It's okay, sweetie. We understand. Jacob can be very persuasive."

That was true, but that wasn't the problem.

"But..."

Mom stepped forward and wrapped her arm around my shoulders. "Come on, Ava. Let his mom take care of it."

I turned to stare at her. How could she just stand by and let this happen? It was ridiculous. She had to know that. "Mom?"

Mom gave me a stern look. One that said, *I'm not going to argue about this.*

I sighed and turned back to the door just to find Jacob and Mrs. Stephenson were gone. When I glanced back and saw Mom's sympathetic look, I lost it.

My body began to shake. Maybe it was because of my anger. I suddenly felt really cold, and my knees buckled under me. Mom had to help me limp over to the bed.

"Ava," Mom said, helping me to sit down. "What's going on?"

I sank onto the comforter. I paused for a moment to gather my strength, and then I turned to her. "What's the matter with you?" I asked.

Mom pulled back a bit to study me. "What are you talking about?"

I scoffed. She was so good at playing naive. "How can you let Mrs. Stephenson talk about Jacob like that?" I leaned toward her. "I kissed Jacob. Me." I thrust my finger at my chest.

There. It had taken me a minute, but I finally found my voice. If only Jacob had been around to hear it.

CHAPTER ELEVEN

Mom studied me for a moment and then sighed. "Really?" she asked.

I stared at her. How come everyone was so convinced that Jacob was this crazy hooligan? Going around and converting everyone to his life of crime? Was I the only one who remembered all the good things he'd done before this whole gas station thing went down?

"Of course, Mom! What do you think? He coerced me into kissing him?" I sighed. "You were the one who was encouraging us to kiss downstairs under the mistletoe. But, what? Now that there is no ridiculous competition, it's suddenly a bad thing to do?"

Mom was silent as she watched me. Then she sighed. "You have to understand what's at stake here. Andrew almost lost his scholarship because he was hanging out with Jacob. Now, you?" She waved her hand at me. "You could lose your future if you let guys like Jacob take over your life. You could get…pregnant." Her face paled, and then a stern look crossed over it. "You are not allowed to see Jacob like that again."

I leaned back against the pillows and began to pick at the lint on my shirt. "Mom. Are you serious? I'm not stupid. I'm not going to get pregnant from kissing a guy." I groaned at that thought. I doubted any guy would ever want to get close to me again.

And I was tired of my parents always having to win. "I don't know what's going on between you guys and the Stephensons, but I'm done. I'm not playing these ridiculous games anymore. You've pitted Jacob and Andrew against each other, and now they're not friends. And now with this"—I swung my legs over the side of the bed in a dramatic movement—"you've ruined Christmas."

I didn't wait for Mom to respond. I left Jacob's room and stormed out into the hallway. She was banishing me from Jacob? Was she serious?

Frustration and anger ran through me. Just as I neared my room, Andrew appeared from his doorway. I ran smack dab into his chest.

I pulled back and glared at him. "You," I said in a voice that rivaled the devil.

He raised his eyebrows. "What happened?"

I held my gaze on his face. What a loyal brother. Ha! Where had he been when I'd tried to defend Jacob earlier? Oh, that's right, nowhere. "You're ridiculous, you know that?" I placed my hands on my hips.

His face paled. "What did Jacob say to you?"

I stared at him. "What does that mean? Do you seriously think that Jacob is talking about you behind your back?" I folded my arms. "He's not like that. He's never once said anything bad about you. But you?" I shook my head as I stepped around my brother. "You're way worse than he is."

I opened my bedroom door and flipped on the light. "Whatever happened, you should forgive him," I said as I slammed the door on my brother's startled face.

It felt good for a split second, and then reality fell down around me. Slamming doors on my brother was never going to make me feel better. It didn't erase what had happened.

My Christmas break romance was over. Jacob and I were over.

Every emotion that I had been trying to suppress exploded inside of me. I flung myself onto my bed and buried my face into the covers. Sobs escaped my lips but were muffled in the folds of fabric.

The first guy who kissed me and even remotely thought I was attractive gets run off by both his parents and mine. I should have known that my chance for love just wouldn't work out. I was destined to be a bachelorette the rest of my life.

After I had no more tears left to cry, I flipped onto my back and stared up at the underside of the bed above me. Even though I hated myself for thinking about Jacob, I couldn't help it. He had occupied my thoughts for so long that I wasn't sure I knew who I was without him.

What was he doing? Was he thinking about me?

Ugh.

I grabbed a nearby pillow and covered my face with it.

One thing was for sure, he probably wasn't obsessing about our situation like I was. He'd probably already forgotten about me.

And then I thought about his mom. And about my mom. And how much I hated the fact that our parents had dragged us here and forced us to compete. This was ridiculous. They shouldn't treat us this way.

I spent the rest of the night in my room alone. I could hear games getting played in the living room, but I didn't care. I was going to stay here until all the merriment died down.

The next morning, I woke up just as frustrated as I had been the night before. Nothing—not even sleep—could make me feel better. It was like someone had reached into my chest and pulled out my heart.

Every part of me hurt.

I groaned as I turned to my side and hugged my chest. Self-pity boiled up inside of me. I let that anger fuel me as I stood up and got dressed. I was done with this stupid competition, and I

RULE #4 YOU CAN'T MISINTERPRET A MISTLETOE KISS | 81

was recruiting the twins and Max to my cause. Tomorrow was Christmas Eve, and I was ready to start celebrating my own way. After I threw my hair up into a ponytail, I grabbed the door handle and turned it, a new sense of purpose coming over me.

I was sick of never having any fun. Of always going along with my parents because I didn't want to make waves. Well, I wanted to make waves. I was going to show them just how Ava Rogers competed.

I walked over to the twin's door. They were, once again, wrestling inside of the room. I knocked on the door. After a few shushes, I heard Alex call out, "Who's there?"

I swung the door open to find them red-faced and sweaty, but trying to look as if they hadn't just been roughhousing in the house that my mom was desperate to keep the cleaning deposit on, "for heaven's sake."

"Ready for some real Christmas fun?" I asked, folding my arms and wiggling my eyebrows.

They studied me.

"What exactly are you thinking?" Aiden asked.

I gave him a sly smile and rubbed my hands together. "You'll just have to come with me to find out."

I grumbled at Aiden, who was forming a snowball and getting ready to chuck it at Max. For some reason, I thought it would be fun to gather them together in their snow gear and lug them out to the Christmas tree grove to cut down a tree just for us to decorate.

They, of course, were on board. A chance to use a gigantic axe of death would convert any ten-year-old boy. But now that we actually had to drag the tree back to the house, they were suddenly way too tired.

"Aiden!" I yelled as he let go of the snowball, sending it whizzing past me.

He glanced over and shrugged. "Sorry. Max was right behind you."

I shot him a death glare, but if he saw, he didn't care. He dive-bombed a snow pile just as he was pelted with snowballs.

Suddenly, the story of the little red hen rolled through my mind. I rolled my eyes as I kept my gaze on the house. I had to do this. I had to show those ridiculous parents of ours just what Christmas spirit meant.

And hopefully forget my broken heart.

When I neared the kitchen window, I made the mistake of glancing up. Jacob was standing just on the other side. He was watching me with a semi-amused expression on his face.

I glared at him and then turned away. Why didn't he look as miserable as I felt? Had I been the only one who'd cared? Even though he had been the first one to say he liked me, it felt like I was the only one who'd meant it.

"Aiden. Alex," I said as I turned to find my brothers with snow covering every inch of their bodies.

"What?" Max asked, coming up behind them.

"Help me." I figured a commanding voice was the only way to get them to do anything.

They sighed very loudly, but complied.

After about half the needles were knocked off, we finally lugged the tree into the house and propped it against the wall. Then I helped excavate them from their snow gear.

We'd made such a huge ruckus that everyone in the house—including Jacob—came into the living room to see what we were doing.

"What's that?" Andrew asked as he leaned against the wall with a cup of hot cocoa in his hand.

I slipped off my boots and waved toward the tree. "Oh this? I'm glad you asked. This is *our* Christmas tree. The boys and I are

RULE #4 YOU CAN'T MISINTERPRET A MISTLETOE KISS | 83

boycotting this ridiculous need for competition. We have decided to do our own Christmas."

The twins and Max all whooped and hollered while I gave a flourishing bow.

"What?" Mom asked.

I turned to her, anger building up inside of me. "We're done with your competition and being told what to do." I sent a pointed look in her direction. "We're done with making sure our family wins. We just want to have fun and not worry if we frost a cookie wrong or our gingerbread house falls flat."

Not waiting for her response, I turned to the three eager boys behind me. "Go find any toy you want. We'll use it as a Christmas ornament. I'll find a stand."

They didn't wait for me to release them. They all bolted off in different directions, each yelling about what toy they were going to get.

Tracy was snapping pictures as they sprinted past. When she peered out from behind the camera, she gave me a small smile. "Can I add something?"

I nodded. "Of course."

She snapped a few other photos and then disappeared upstairs with a spring in her step.

"So, now we'll have four Christmas trees?" Mr. Stephenson asked.

I just gave him a small smile. "Yep. And two different Christmases if you adults don't get your act together."

I didn't wait for anyone to ask any more questions. I needed to find a Christmas tree stand before the boys returned and started piling their toys wherever they could find a spot.

I kept my gaze on the floor as I walked past the spectators—including Jacob—and made my way into the garage, hoping to find a stand tucked away on a shelf.

After propping a ladder precariously against the storage shelves along the far wall, I started shifting through the cardboard boxes. Some had Easter decorations. Others were full of pumpkins and scarecrows.

"Ah, come on," I said, grumbling under my breath.

"Need a hand?"

A shiver rushed down my spine as Jacob's voice broke the silence. Not wanting to turn around and look into his ridiculously mesmerizing eyes and stupidly handsome face, I kept my head buried in the Halloween box that I was balancing on the edge of the shelf.

"No," I finally muttered. I closed my eyes for a second, praying that he would go away. "And I don't think you're allowed to be in here. We've been forbidden to see each other."

I paused, and when he didn't answer, I let my shoulders relax. Thank goodness that was over. I shifted slightly on the ladder and suddenly, I found myself falling.

Scrambling to save myself, I tried to free my hand from the box, but the stringy spider web clung to me, and I couldn't shake myself free.

I screamed as I fell backwards. There was nothing I could do. I was going to die.

I braced myself for the impact, but it never came.

Instead, two very strong and very familiar arms wrapped around me and halted my descent. Jacob was holding me. Of course he was. It was just my luck.

"You okay?" Jacob asked, his annoyingly sexy voice sending unwanted ripples of excitement through my body.

"Yeah, um-hum," I said as I struggled to stand.

Jacob seemed to sense my rush to get out of his arms and helped me the rest of the way. Once I was upright, I nodded toward him.

"Thanks for...that." What was I supposed to say? Thanks for rescuing me even though just an hour earlier, our parents were forcing us apart and you seemed totally okay with that?

He nodded and looked away. "You're welcome."

I glanced behind him. "Where's your mom? Are you sure you can be seen talking to me? After all, my mom thinks you're going to get me pregnant from kissing me." Heat rushed over my cheeks as I realized what I had just said.

A hurt expression flashed across his face. "She said what?"

I rolled my shoulders, hoping to lessen the tension in them. "Apparently, my parents think you're this horrible influence that's going to take my virtue and leave me pregnant."

His forehead furrowed. "They do?"

I sighed and shook my hand free of the spider webs. "Yeah, but I know none of that is true." I eyed him, waiting for some indication that I was right.

He did look relieved, but then his defeated expression returned. "Maybe they're right."

I was so frustrated, words were no longer forming in my mind. I needed to speak now before I lost my nerve. "Jacob, what the heck are you talking about? They aren't right. You're not some guy running around and getting girls pregnant. That's ridiculous. And I'm sick of you letting people believe that about you."

He pushed his hands through his hair as he studied the cement. "You think you know me—"

I sighed so loud that he stopped talking. He glanced up at me as he shoved his hands into his front pockets.

"I can't help you, Jacob. If you want people to believe that about you, then fine. We're done. Nothing can happen between us with the way things are." I gave him a weary smile. "And if that's what you want, it's what I want."

Plus, fighting with him didn't feel very Christmasy. If I wanted to bring back the spirit of this holiday, arguing with him would put me on the naughty list.

"Only you can fix this, Jacob," I said, hating that I sounded like my mom. I turned and studied the boxes in front of me. There was a straggler at the end marked *Christmas Decorations*.

I grabbed the ladder and pulled it over. Just as I started to climb, Jacob held out his hand.

"I'll do it," he said.

Feelings of hurt, frustration, and excitement rushed through me as I felt the tips of his fingers pressed against my arm. I wanted to run from him, shake him, and kiss him, all at the same time. But, I did none of those. I didn't want him to know how much this whole situation between us was affecting me. Plus, he was still here, even after my rant. That had to mean something.

So I shrugged and moved back. "Fine."

He climbed the ladder, and I forced my gaze to remain on the cement floor at my feet. I hated the way his jeans clung to his legs. It just wasn't fair.

After rifling around in the box for a minute or two, he turned and held out a tree stand. "This work?" he asked.

I nodded. "That's perfect." Once Jacob was down, I took the stand from him and turned to head back into the house.

"Hey, Ava," Jacob said. I couldn't help it; I stopped in my tracks.

"Yeah?" I closed my eyes, praying and hoping that he'd say something about what had happened in his room yesterday.

"I have an idea."

CHAPTER TWELVE

"I freakin' love this!" Aiden exclaimed as he jumped around our tree, pumping his fists. He paused to chest bump Alex and Max, who had the same look of joy on their faces. They were busy hanging ghosts and pumpkins across the tree's branches. Tiny skeleton lights blinked through the spider webs they'd strung.

I laughed and reached out to tousle his hair. "It was a pretty good idea, huh?" My gaze made its way over to Jacob where he leaned against the far wall, right beside the fireplace.

The roaring fire lit up his face, and I could see the satisfaction there. When he looked up and caught me staring, heat flushed my skin. And when he winked, I wanted to melt into a puddle on the floor.

And then, as if he realized that he'd just winked at me, his face went stony and he dropped his eyes.

My heart plummeted. He really knew how to bolster and then break a girl in a matter of seconds.

When I turned my attention back to the tree, I scolded myself. There was no reason why one look from Jacob should do anything to me. We were never going to work out. I needed to accept that. If he wasn't going to fight for us, neither would I.

"Here, let me," I said, stepping forward and grabbing the witch that Max was trying to throw to the top of the tree.

"It's the star," he said.

I laughed and placed the witch riding a broomstick where the star would normally go. She had no stand, so she looked as if she were dive-bombing the tree.

"What do you think?" Max asked.

I smiled over at him. "It's perfect."

Tracy stepped up from behind Max and snapped a picture. I tried to smile in time, but I think I missed it. Hoping that she didn't get me making a weird face, I eyed her.

"Tracy," I said, I really wished she would put the camera down and just join in.

Tracy just glanced at her camera and shrugged.

Mom and Dad walked in, followed by the Stephensons. Their expressions were somber, and they looked as if they were ready to have *a talk*.

"Kids, can you sit down?" Mrs. Stephenson asked.

I glared at her—I tried not to, but that woman made me really mad.

The others didn't seem to mind and instantly rushed to fight over who got to sit on the couch. Once they were situated, Mrs. Stephenson glanced over at me. I decided to remain by the tree. I wasn't sure what she was going to say or if I wanted to hear it.

I was still boycotting their version of Christmas.

Mom rubbed her shoulder as she studied us. "We talked and realized that maybe we might have lost the true meaning of Christmas in all of our competitions. What started out as a silly game has gotten"—she sucked her breath in between her teeth—"out of hand."

I scoffed. *That's one way to put it.* Mom furrowed her brow, but didn't say anything further.

RULE #4 YOU CAN'T MISINTERPRET A MISTLETOE KISS | 89

"We want you to realize that what's most important is not winning, but the fact that we do these things together." Mom glanced over at me and gave me a small smile.

I sighed and folded my arms. I really didn't want to give into them this easily. "So, we get to do what we want?"

Mrs. Stephenson stepped forward and furrowed her brow. "Within reason." Her comment was so direct, her gaze boring into me, that I raised my eyebrows.

Was she talking about Jacob and me? Was she telling me that we, as a couple, were still off limits?

Great.

Mom clapped her hands and rubbed them together. She told us that after lunch, we were going to decorate the gingerbread houses.

Aiden piped up, "Any way we want?"

A grimace crossed Mom's face, but then she nodded. "Any way you want, buddy."

I kept to the back part of the room while everyone piled into the kitchen. I could hear the fridge opening and closing and plates getting set on the counter. I was hungry, but if I were honest with myself, I really didn't want to spend time with my family.

Not when my heart was broken from the way they were acting toward me and Jacob. The fact that they still saw us as the wrong type of couple made me angry. Jacob was a good kid. Why couldn't they see that?

When Andrew didn't head into the kitchen, I zeroed in on him. He kept his gaze on his phone as I stood in front of him, tapping my foot.

"What do you want, Ava?"

I placed my hands on my hips and dipped down so he had to look at me.

He sighed and clicked the power button on his phone and then slipped it into his pocket.

"We need to talk." I turned, hoping he'd follow me, and headed into the small office next to the stairs. Once we were inside, I shut the doors and turned to face him.

He looked uncomfortable but was trying not to as he awkwardly leaned against the desk. "What do you want?" he asked again. This time without his normal confidence.

"Spill," I said.

His face paled as he glanced toward the bookshelves on one side of the room and then squinted toward the open window on the other side. "I don't know what you're talking about."

I groaned as I glared at him. "We are best friends. We tell each other everything. There is something going on in this house that you aren't talking about, and it's killing any hope I have to be with Jacob." Just as the words left my lips, tears formed on my lids. My heart was hemorrhaging in my chest. I was a fool to think that I could just move on from Jacob unscathed.

And now that he was back from his grandmother's and coming to school in a few weeks, I was screwed. There was no way I could go to the same school as him. See him in the halls—most likely flirting with other girls—and be okay. And it was so selfish of my brother to inflict that on me.

He sighed. "You don't get it." He paused, and I could see the internal conflict in his eyes. "There's nothing to tell. Last summer happened the way the judge said it did. There's nothing that can be done." He winced as he met my gaze. "You're better than him, Ava. Move on." He looked at the floor. "Please?"

I studied him. Sure, my brother was trying to appear sincere, but I knew him better than he gave me credit for. He was lying. I could see it in his snaky gaze. And it made my blood boil. My brother saw my misery, and yet he still wasn't being honest with me. He could fix this problem, but he wouldn't.

But I couldn't force him to tell the truth, so I sighed and slumped against the wall. "Fine. Suit yourself." After a moment to compose myself, I glared over at him. "But if you think I'll ever have your back after this, think again." I paused, just to let that sink in, and then opened the office door and made my way out.

I ignored the look Jacob gave me as I passed by him and entered the kitchen, sitting down next to Aiden and Alex. I was ready to start celebrating Christmas. I was done with both of those ridiculous boys. They could keep their stupid secrets and their misery. I was ready to move on.

"Hey, Ava," Aiden said grinning over at me, exposing the blue frosting that he'd just squeezed into his mouth.

I shot him a disgusted look but then laughed. And it felt good. Like, really good. I needed to feel free. After being under the suffocating weight of the competition and the burden of whatever Jacob and Andrew were carrying, I was ready to let my hair down and just have fun.

Tracy, Aiden, Alex, and Max were chatting at the table as we assembled the gingerbread houses. Aiden and Alex wanted to continue with the Halloween theme and create zombies and skeletons with Christmas hats with the leftover gingerbread dough. I saw the internal battle going on as the parents bit back their protests and just let it happen.

A few times, Tracy got up and snapped some pictures. We laughed. We talked. We listened to Christmas music. And for the first time this vacation, I was happy.

Jacob and Andrew didn't come into the room, and I was okay with that. The air felt lighter when they weren't around.

After the gingerbread houses were decorated and sitting on the counter to dry, I grinned at the boys and asked them if they wanted to have a snowball fight. They cheered and scrambled to be the first to get their snow gear on.

Thankfully, Mom and Mrs. Stephenson looked as if they were ready for a break, so they helped me dress the hooligans.

Tracy came down the stairs in her snow gear just as I pulled my gloves onto my hands. I eyed her. "Coming?" I asked.

She nodded and then pulled her phone from her pocket. "I've

got to document everything, right?"

I smiled as I pulled open the front door and released the spastic boys. "You do know you're entering a war zone. All is fair out here," I said as I bounded down the front steps.

She followed after me. "I'm counting on it."

Thirty minutes later, I was hiding behind a tree, trying my hardest to get a good stockpile of snowballs. We'd divided into groups. Aiden and I were against Alex and Max. Tracy was the damsel we were trying to save from the forest beast and the opposing team.

It was an elaborate story that the boys came up with. Since I didn't want to go back inside, I'd agreed to play along. Now, it was out of desperation to stay alive. One thing was for certain, these boys didn't play around. They meant business.

Voices drew my attention over toward the trees. They were low and angry, and they definitely didn't sound like ten-year-old boys. I paused, trying to catch what was being said.

"This has to end."

Wait. Was that Jacob?

Now I was intrigued. I set down the snowball I was forming and scooted toward a nearby tree, crouching down behind the trunk. I peeked around to find Jacob standing in the snow with only a jacket on—of course. Andrew was standing in front of him with his hands buried in the front pocket of his sweatshirt. His hood was over his head, and his gaze turned toward the snow.

"Why? It's over. Can't you people just move on?" He raised his face toward the sky and let his breath out slowly.

"I didn't care before. What happened, happened. But now, things have changed."

My heart skipped a beat as I shifted so I could read Jacob's face. His eyes were narrowed, and there was a pained expression there.

"You mean, Ava?" Andrew scoffed. "Come on, you always said she was my dorky younger sister. She's just a conquest for you. Someone you can't have." I could see Andrew's face grow frustrated as he met Jacob's gaze. "You can't tell me that this has anything to do with her. All you wanted was for your parents to send you to your grandmother's. That was the deal." He pulled off his hoodie. "Things not work out with Michelle?"

My stomach, which had lightened from Jacob's words, suddenly felt like a lead weight had dropped inside of it. Who was Michelle? Why hadn't Jacob said anything about her?

My hands shook inside of my gloves as I clung to the tree trunk for support. I felt so mad and betrayed I could barely keep myself upright. I wanted to confront them, but this was the most truth I'd heard from either of them, so I waited.

"She's gone. We're done." Jacob blew into his hands and then shoved them into his front pockets.

"And you think moving on with my kid sister is a good idea? Geez, Jacob. That's the stupidest idea I've heard from you in a long time."

Great. Now I was his kid sister. A dork. A knife felt like it was slicing through my stomach at his words. Sure, Jacob wasn't saying those things, but he wasn't defending me either.

It was really eye-opening to stand in the shadows and hear what they thought about me. Here, I'd allowed myself to believe that Jacob cared about me and that my brother respected me. And yet, I had been completely wrong. And it hurt. So bad.

"Enough. I don't need your permission or our parents' permission. I'm just ready for the truth to be told." Jacob met Andrew's gaze, and I could see the annoyance written all over his face.

Andrew scoffed. "Too late. That was part of the deal. You'd take the fall for me and get shipped off to grandma's house. I get off and keep my scholarship. I'm sorry things didn't work out for you, but they're working out for me."

I stared at Andrew. Jacob took the fall for him?

Jacob let out a growl. "What you asked wasn't right. You were the one who stole, not me. You knew I was mad at my parents, and I was ready to do just about anything to get out from under them." Jacob flexed his hands as if he were trying to get some feeling back in them. "You were supposed to be my friend."

Andrew shrugged. "Well, I can't rewrite the past." He dropped his head and turned. "Sorry it didn't work out for you." His boots crunched in the snow as he started back toward the house.

I wasn't going to let him get away this easy, I chased after him.

When I caught up to Andrew, I could barely keep my tears at bay. "So that was the truth?" I asked.

So much was happening in such a short period of time, and I was struggling to keep my emotions in check.

Andrew turned, his eyes wide. "What?" He glanced behind me. "Were you eavesdropping?"

I glared at him. "You let Jacob go down for the gas station thing? It was you all along?"

Andrew's face paled, and his gaze turned desperate. "You don't understand." He scrubbed his face with his hand. "Mom and Dad put so much stress on me to perform. To be perfect at everything." He stepped closer to me. "You get it. They do the same to you."

I stepped back, not wanting to be that close to him. "Yeah, but I don't steal stuff and then make my best friend take the fall for me. And..." Despite my best effort, a sob escaped my lips. I composed myself and tried again. "And you looked me in the eye and told me that what the judge said was true. You knew I was hurting, and you could have fixed it, but you didn't."

For the first time, I truly felt betrayed by my brother. He was supposed to be my ally. My best friend. And beyond that, he was my family. Family didn't do this to each other.

"What are you going to do?" he asked. His voice was low.

I glared at him. "What you should have done a long time ago." I walked past him toward the house. "Tell the truth."

CHAPTER THIRTEEN

I sat at the table, pushing some stray sprinkles around with my finger. I could hear the low murmurs from the front room as my parents, the Stephensons, Andrew, and Jacob talked.

The boys and Tracy were downstairs watching a show. They were bummed that they had to come inside before they finished their snowball fight, but when they were promised candy and a movie, they changed their tune.

I was so nervous that I decided to camp in the kitchen.

After talking with Andrew, I'd rushed into the house like a tornado out of hell. Everything had spilled from me like vomit, leaving all the adults in the room a little whiplashed.

After I'd finished, I stood there shaking. Partly from the cold, and partly from the emotions rushing through me.

Now they were all sitting in the living room, and I couldn't make out what was being said. But from the low tones of their voices, no one was very happy.

"I mean, this is just ridiculous," Mrs. Stephenson said as she came barreling into the kitchen and opened the fridge, Mr. Stephenson following close behind. "We've been made out to be these terrible, unloving parents, when all along, it's their child who's the criminal." She pulled out a bottle of white wine and popped the cork.

"I know, JoAnne, I'm disappointed too."

She filled a wine glass to the brim and shot Mr. Stephenson a look as she downed half of it. "And he got the promotion over you. They walk around like they're the better people." She finished that glass and poured another. "I'm just...ugh." She started gulping the wine again.

I could see that Mr. Stephenson wanted to stop her, but didn't know how.

Finally he sighed. "What do you want to do?"

She finished the wine and set the glass down on the counter. "I can't stay here." She sighed as she rubbed her temples. "We're leaving."

I parted my lips. I wanted to protest. Max and Tracy didn't deserve to have their Christmas cut short. And truthfully, neither did they.

Sure, they'd based their relationship with my parents on competition, but they had to see this as a win. Their son had been kind to his friend in a messed up and weird sort of way. I muscled down the memory of Andrew talking about Michelle. This wasn't about my feelings for Jacob anymore. This was about healing our families.

But the Stephensons left the kitchen before I could gather my thoughts together.

They must have told my parents they were leaving, Mom and Dad's faces were solemn as they moved around the kitchen. I wasn't sure what Mom was doing because she started taking random food out of the fridge and bowls from the cupboards.

Just as she was about to pour salad into the bowl with pasta sauce, Dad stopped her.

"What are you doing?" he asked, wrapping her up into a hug.

Mom sobbed into his shoulder. "They hate us. It's over," she said.

Regret formed in my gut. I did feel bad for spilling the story, but it had to be told.

"I'm sorry, Mom," I said as I stood up from the table and made my way over.

Mom pulled back and shook her head. "No. It's not your fault. It's ours. We shouldn't have..." She closed her eyes and winced. "We were bad parents."

Now I really felt bad. I reached out and hugged her. "No you're not. You're not bad parents. Look at me. I turned out okay."

Mom laughed and cupped my cheek with her hand.

"And there's still time for the twins." As much as they bugged me, I did love my little brothers.

Mom nodded.

"And Andrew's just a little misguided right now. He's just going through something. But we won't give up on him." My heart swelled a bit. Even though I was hurt, I still loved my brother.

Mom gave me a small smile as she blotted her cheeks. "Thank you, Ava. You know how to make me feel better."

I nodded. "And it's not over. After all, it's Christmas." I smiled. "I'll go talk to the Stephensons."

A worried look passed over Mom's face, and I just shook my head. She shouldn't be worried. We were just two broken families trying to figure out our mistakes.

I patted Mom's hand and turned, making my way toward the stairs. I made my way up to the second floor. When I got to the landing, I could hear a ruckus coming from the Stephensons' room. Drawers were opening and closing, and Mrs. Stephenson kept repeating "I just can't believe it."

Just as I walked past Jacob's room, a hand reached out and grabbed my arm. Seconds later, I found myself inside of Jacob's room as he was shutting the door.

Butterflies assaulted my stomach as the memory of yesterday

came rushing back to me. I forced them to still—unsuccessfully—and turned to face Jacob.

"What do you want?" I asked, folding my arms.

His expression was strained as he turned to look at me. "Why did you do that?"

Frustration burned my skin. "What? I told the truth. Which is something you and my brother seem to fail at."

Jacob scrubbed his face. "I couldn't tell you. It would ruin Andrew. He was going to lose his scholarship. I…"

I narrowed my eyes. "And you were going to lose your flirty time with Michelle?"

He winced as he dropped his gaze to the floor. "You heard that, huh?"

I sighed and moved toward the door. There was no way I wanted to stay here any longer. I was barely hanging onto my strength as it was, there was no way I wanted to bring up Jacob's girlfriend, or make-out buddy, or whatever this Michelle was to him.

"I don't care anymore, Jacob"—that was a lie—"I'm just going to try to fix what you two did before our parents decide to hate each other forever." I pulled open the door and looked back. "And just in case you didn't pick up on it, this dorky, kid sister is done."

I made my way out into the hall and shut the door behind me. Once I was alone, I closed my eyes. I was shaking inside and out. My heart was breaking inside of my chest, but what else was I supposed to do? Let him back in?

Even though my heart was screaming yes, I decided to listen to my head, which was saying, "are you an idiot?"

So I straightened my shoulders and headed into the Stephensons' room.

Mrs. Stephenson was on the bed, blotting her eyes, as Mr. Stephenson was packing the suitcase next to her. His lips were pulled into a tight line.

When they saw me, they gave me a small smile.

"Hey, Ava," Mr. Stephenson said and then disappeared into the closet.

Mrs. Stephenson wiped her nose and patted the bed. "Ava." Her voice was crackly and she looked tired.

I joined her, turning slightly so I could look at her. "How's it going?" I asked. I don't know why I asked that. I knew exactly how she was doing. I could tell by the look on her face.

She shrugged, blew her nose, and crumpled up the tissue to send it sailing into the garbage. "I've been better." She sighed. "I just wish things had been different, you know?"

Not sure what to do, I reached out and patted her hand. It felt weird, so I pulled my arm back and settled for resting my hands on my lap. "You don't have to go," I said.

Mrs. Stephenson let out a small laugh. "Oh, honey, I wish it were that simple."

It broke my heart a bit that everyone was suffering this much from something that happened so many months ago. Sure, it was a big deal when it was keeping Jacob and I apart, but I was so naive—crap, Jacob had been right—I didn't realize how much this whole situation had been straining our parents during this entire vacation.

I'm sure it was hard to be the parent of the delinquent child as much as it was hard to be the parent of the victim. They were carrying this weight around on their shoulders before the truth even came out.

"It wasn't fair," I whispered.

Mrs. Stephenson pulled out another tissue and sniffed as she wiped her nose. "What did you say?"

"It wasn't fair. Any of it." I met her gaze. "You felt guilty about Jacob being the one to drag Andrew into doing something illegal. And you shouldered that guilt every time we got together." Realization dawned on me. "So when you saw Jacob and I kissing, you felt as if he was trying to corrupt me too."

A tear slid down Mrs. Stephenson's face. She nodded and

wiped the tear with the tips of her fingers. "Our life changed when Jacob was accused. Dirk didn't get the promotion. People treated us differently."

I nodded. "That had to be hard."

She patted my hands. "Yes. But that's not something you should worry about."

I shook my head. "But it is. Now, my parents are about to go through the same thing. Even though you are no longer at fault, you can't tell me that you want your best friends to do this alone?"

Wow. For a seventeen-year-old, I surprised even myself.

Mrs. Stephenson was studying me and then scoffed. "When did you get so wise?" she asked, wiping her nose.

I shrugged. "I'm just that kind of girl."

We fell silent for a moment before I glanced back over to her. "Please stay. My parents need you. Our family needs your family. Don't let a stupid decision made by stupid boys ruin Christmas."

Her expression softened. Good. I was wearing her down.

"Plus Tracy and Max don't deserve to be punished. They are having a lot of fun."

She sighed and leaned back onto the pillows behind her. She was turning the tissue around and around in her hands. "I don't know..." she whispered.

I stood. "I do. Trust me. Staying is the best present you could ever give my parents." I gave her sly look. "One could say it would be a present that could never be beat."

Her expression brightened at bit at that statement. I wanted to roll my eyes. Just mention competition and the Stephensons suddenly perked right up. But, I wasn't going to say anything. If that was what fixed their relationship with my parents, then I'd let it be.

As I made my way out of the room, Mrs. Stephenson called out my name. I turned to find her smiling at me.

"I'm sorry for what I said about you and Jacob." She crumpled the tissue in her hand again. "I was wrong to treat you two that

RULE #4 YOU CAN'T MISINTERPRET A MISTLETOE KISS | 101

way." She sighed. "But the more I get to know you, the more I realize that you really are too good for Jacob."

My stomach flipped at her confession. Was she giving us her blessing?

I just smiled as I slipped out into the hall. It didn't matter. Jacob and I were done. No matter what happened between the Stephensons and the Rogers, Jacob and I could never be.

He'd broken my heart, and I wasn't sure how that would ever be fixed.

I walked into my bedroom to find Tracy sitting on the bed. In all the drama, she must have left the boys downstairs. She had her camera in her hand and was staring at the screen.

She glanced up at me. There was a sad look in her eye.

I gave her an encouraging smile, but that didn't seem to fix anything. "You okay?" I asked.

Tracy shrugged. "Just looking over the photos I took."

I moved over to sit next to her on the bed. "Oh yeah? Can I see?"

She tipped the camera toward me and started flipping through them. The ones that were taken of our parents and their trees felt stiff and strained. I could feel the stress permeating off of them.

Then there were ones of Jacob and me. Where we were leaning against the wall or stringing popcorn. We looked so…relaxed. So comfortable with each other. My heart ached at the sight.

Even though I'd just told him moments ago that I wanted nothing to do with him, I missed him.

Then she got to the photos of us decorating our Halloween tree. The twins and Max looked so happy, jumping around. I smiled as she paused on one where I was open-mouth laughing. Even my parents looked somewhat happy.

"These are great, Tracy," I said.

She shrugged. "Good. Because these are the ones I just submitted to the show."

I glanced over at her. "Wow. Nice." I wrapped my arm around

her shoulders, suddenly feeling sad that I hadn't hung out with her this entire trip. "I like your style."

She shrugged. "I liked what you did with the parents. Someone needed to shine some light on their ridiculousness." Then she gave me a shy smile. "And you're good for Jacob. I hope you two figure something out."

My stomach twisted at her words. "Thanks, Tracy."

CHAPTER FOURTEEN

My parents were overjoyed when the Stephensons decided to stay through the holiday. I smiled as they hugged and cried—well, the moms cried. They said they were sorry for everything and from this moment on, they were going to be better friends.

They also glared at Jacob and Andrew and told them that after Christmas was over, they were going to make things right. Andrew dipped his head and nodded. Jacob did the same.

We spent Christmas Eve alternating between making sugar cookies and wrapping presents. Those who were in the kitchen filled the time by talking about what we wanted Santa to bring us.

It was cute to watch Alex and Aiden stare each other down as they tried to decide whether Santa was real or not. I nodded and told them I'd seen Santa before, which they completely believed. After a few minutes, they declared him real and rushed off to start making their lists.

I chuckled as Tracy got out her camera and started snapping photos of them sitting at the table. I met her gaze and smiled. We still hadn't told anyone that she'd already submitted the photos.

They were announcing the winner at six, so we were just waiting until then.

I kind of doubted that our parents really even cared about that anymore.

Plus, it helped me attempt to ignore the fact that I missed Jacob. Like. A lot.

I missed talking to him. Flirting with him. I just missed everything. And I wanted him back. Sure, I knew I should be mad with him, but I couldn't help it. After a good night sleep and a hot shower, I'd already forgiven him.

I wasn't like my family. I forgave easily. And maybe the soft Christmas music carrying through the house, mixed with lots of hot chocolate, made me a more relaxed person. It was probably what made Santa so jolly.

The Christmas song playing on the radio faded, and the DJ came back on. He said something about the contest and the number of entries. My ears perked up, and I shushed the other people in the room.

Mrs. Stephenson glanced over at me with a quizzical expression.

"Guys, listen," I said.

"After much deliberation, we have a winner," the DJ proclaimed.

"We missed the deadline, Ava," Mom said.

I just shook my head and pressed my finger to my lips. A move she should recognize, since she created it.

"We have to say, we got lots of photos of perfect Christmas trees and impeccable cookies, but this one blew them all out of the water. Even though they didn't use conventional decorations, you could tell that they showed real Christmas spirit."

There was a drumroll.

"The Rogers and the Stephenson clan took the gold! Congrats to your families. I have to say, those three boys showed the most Christmas spirit as they decorated that tree."

I glanced around, grinning from ear to ear. My brothers and Max were jumping up and down. I was pretty sure they didn't understand what they'd just won, but they were excited that people liked their tree.

Mom stared at me. "Did you send the pictures in?"

I shook my head. "Nope. Tracy did."

The parents were silent as they glanced at each other. Suddenly, my mom wrapped an arm around my shoulders. "I'm sorry for everything, Ava."

I turned to hug her. "I know, Mom."

The parents were so humbled that they let the boys eat half of the cookies before they cut them off. Then they went to the basement to watch a Christmas movie and play.

I was in such a good mood that I agreed to help Mrs. Stephenson clean up the dirty dishes as the cookies cooled on the counter. Apparently, no matter if there was a competition or not, I still wasn't allowed to touch the food. Instead, I got clean up duty, which I was fine with. I wanted the cookies to be edible. If I baked them, they'd be as hard as bricks.

Halfway through the dishes, Mrs. Stephenson got a phone call from her mom, so I told her I could finish up. Now alone, I watched the bubbles swirl around as I ran the dishcloth through them.

A warm arm brushing mine drew my attention over. Despite the warmth of the water, my hands suddenly became cold. Jacob was standing next to me with a towel in one hand and a sheepish expression on his face.

"I hope this is okay," he said, peeking over at me.

I shrugged but didn't say anything. In fact, I hadn't spoken to him or Andrew since this whole thing went down.

He sighed. "Thanks for talking to my parents."

I nodded and began scrubbing the mixing bowl.

He was quiet for a minute. Then he spoke again. "It was really nice of you to pick up the pieces from the mess Andrew and I created."

I nodded again, still silent.

He reached out and stilled my hand. "Are you not talking to me now?"

I pinched my lips together as warmth radiated up my arm. I wanted to say yes. I wanted to tell him that I hated the way he'd treated me. I was the innocent victim here. I was the one to have my heart broken when I'd done nothing wrong. I wanted to tell him to leave me alone and never talk to me again.

But the ache in my chest grew deeper and more painful. I didn't really want any of those things.

"Jacob," I whispered, braving the pain. "You hurt me."

His features stilled as he nodded. "I know." He ran his hands through his hair. "You deserve someone so much better than me. If you tell me to leave you alone, I'll respect that." He hesitated as if he were waiting for me to wave my hand and banish him from my sight.

Which, I'm not going to lie, I kind of wanted to do.

He raised his hand just as I parted my lips. "Can I explain something first?"

I eyed him and then nodded, waving my soapy hand to tell him to continue.

"I was an idiot last summer. I'd met a girl at my grandmother's, and we kind of hit it off. My parents were driving me crazy, and I wanted to get away. When I went out with Andrew, and he decided to do something stupid, I made a snap judgement. I figured I'd take the fall—because people thought it was my fault anyway—and get to spend some time with my grandma. Andrew would be able to keep his scholarship, and everything would be fine."

When he stepped closer to me, my heart picked up speed. Suddenly, his gaze intensified. "I didn't know you'd be caught in the crossfire. I never meant for this to happen like it did."

A shiver rushed down my back from the emotion I could hear in his voice.

"Ava, you're not a dork, and you are not stupid. You are the sweetest, kindest, most gentle person I've ever met. I'm shocked that you even consider me as someone worthy of you."

I swallowed as my gaze grew hazy. Did he mean that?

"Jacob—" I began to whisper, but he shook his head.

"I know I've lied to you, and there is no reason for you to ever take me back. But, just promise me you'll keep an open mind." He reached out and tucked a strand of hair behind my ear. "Don't write me off."

I stared at him, my heart hammering in my chest. All I could do was nod. "Okay."

He smiled at me, and my whole body flushed. After leaning forward and gently kissing my cheek, he pulled back and readied the dish towel.

"Now, let's get these dishes done."

I somehow managed to get through the dishes without falling to pieces. It was hard, standing next to Jacob for that long. My mind was swimming, and my whole body was reacting to his proximity.

All I wanted to do was turn and wrap my arms around him and kiss him. Call it holiday spirit. Call it a Christmas miracle, but I was ready to forgive him.

And Michelle? Well, he wasn't in Florida, begging for her to forgive him. He was here. With me. Asking me to keep him in the running.

And sure, I wanted to tell him he was the only one in the race, but he'd asked for some time to earn my trust back, so I really hoped he'd start his heroic plans now so we could get to the making up bit.

He smiled at me as he nodded toward the living room. "I can finish up," he said as he grabbed the sprayer and started rinsing out the sink.

I stepped back and nodded, taking the dish towel he handed to me. "Thanks," I said.

He winked at me.

I stood behind him, methodically wiping my hands with the towel. My gaze made its way over to the opening to the living room. And then it landed on that small ball of green leaves.

Mistletoe.

And suddenly, I didn't have to wait until Jacob enacted all of his plans to show me how sorry he was. If I could get him over to the doorway, he'd have to kiss me. Right?

I stepped up next to Jacob and glanced over at him. "Can I show you something?"

He looked at me as he turned off the water. "Show me something?" He glanced behind me. "Sure."

I handed the towel to him, and he dried his hands. After setting it on the counter, I motioned him toward the living room. Once I got to the doorway, I paused.

Jacob held back for a moment and then stepped up right next to me. "What did you want me to see?"

I pointed toward the mistletoe and watched as Jacob raised his gaze.

"Ava," he said. My toes tingled from the depth of his tone.

"Jacob, one thing you need to know about me. I cannot hold a grudge. Sure, you hurt me, but I know it wasn't intentional." I gave him a small smile. "Besides, I think our families have had enough hurt to last us a while."

I reached out and wrapped my arms around his neck and pulled him to me. My lips found his and I didn't hold back. It was as if kissing Jacob fixed everything that had broken in me this Christmas vacation.

Jacob pulled back and studied me. "But, my plans?"

I shrugged as I bit my lip. "You can still do them, but I'm not waiting. I like you. Like, *like you,* like you."

His hands found my waist, and he pulled me closer to him. "You do? Even after all of that?"

He leaned toward me and pressed his lips to my forehead.

I giggled as I tipped my lips up to him. "You'll owe me for a while, but I'm okay with that."

"Then I look forward to showing you how much *I* like you, like you."

Our lips found each other, and as we fell into the rhythm of our kisses, I couldn't help but feel complete. This was what I wanted this Christmas. Families happy and together. Truths finally told. And Jacob.

Mostly Jacob.

He pulled back and glanced down at me. "So, what can I get you for Christmas?"

I pulled a contemplative look and then grinned at him. "Nothing."

His eyebrows shot up. "Really?"

I snuggled into his chest and breathed in the smell of his woodsy cologne. "Yep. I have everything I want."

His arms wrapped around me and pulled me closer. He pressed his lips to the top of my head and whispered. "That makes me happy."

Shivers rushed across my body as I sighed. This was exactly how I wanted to spend the rest of my Christmas break. Wrapped in Jacob's arms, the smell of fresh-baked Christmas cookies wafting through the air, and with my family.

Merry Christmas to me.

EPILOGUE

The roaring muffler drew the attention of everyone making their way into school the day after Christmas break. Mom and Dad were skeptical, but had allowed Jacob to drive me and Andrew. Andrew had protested, but my parents didn't care. Andrew was on house arrest as far as they were concerned. Plus, next week he was meeting with the judge to confess what had really happened.

Jacob parked, and Andrew nodded to us both and got out.

I was sitting in the front seat with butterflies rushing through my body.

A warm hand engulfed mine. "You okay?" Jacob asked.

I turned and gave him an uneasy smile. "I think so. I'm just nervous. There's a lot of girls at school who are not going to be happy when you show up with me."

He leaned over and pressed his lips against mine. "Who cares? I don't." He nuzzled my neck. "I've got you, and that's all that matters."

I took a deep breath, wishing that his words would comfort me, but they didn't. Girls were mean. And if they saw me as moving in on their territory, I was a goner.

He grabbed my backpack and pulled open his door. "Besides, they'll have to face me if I hear anyone talk bad about you."

After he rounded the hood of his car, he fell into step with me. Both of our backpacks were slung over his shoulder as he grabbed my hand and led me to the front doors.

I could feel everyone's stares as we walked past kids in the hall. There were a few whispers and a few students clapping Jacob on the back and welcoming him back.

When we got to his locker, he spun the dial a few times and pulled the door open. After shuffling his books around from his backpack, he straightened. When he saw my expression, his brow furrowed.

"Are you seriously worried?" he asked.

I shrugged. "What if everything only happened because of the magic of Christmas. What if, in the real world, you don't like me?"

He studied me and then scoffed. Suddenly, his hands were around my waist, and he pressed me against the locker.

"Ava Rogers, that's not going to happen." He leaned closer to me and brushed his lips against mine. "You are the best thing to ever happen to me, and I will never let you go." He steadied his gaze as he leaned his forehead against mine. "I love you," he whispered.

My toes tingled at his confession. I wrapped my arms around his neck and crushed my lips to his. When we came up for air, I met his gaze again. "Good. Because I'm not going anywhere. I love you, too."

His arms wrapped around me, and spun me around. Passing students protested—I may have almost kicked a few of them, but I didn't care.

Once he set me down, he tucked my hair behind my ear. "Look up," he said.

I peeked up toward the ceiling.

"There's nothing there," I said.

He grinned. "Exactly. No mistletoe needed." He pressed his lips against mine and then leaned forward. "The magic of Christmas is me and you." He pulled back, wrapped his hand around mine, and guided me down the hallway.

"Now, let's get you to your class before you're tardy and I start hearing again about how I'm a bad influence on you."

I rolled my eyes and fell into step with him. I wrapped my free hand around our entwined ones and sighed.

This was perfect.

***

Want MORE romance?
Grab the first book in the series:
Rule #1: You Can't Date the Coaches Daughter
If only my heart understood the rules, I wouldn't have fallen for Tyson Blake. Stupid heart.
Grab it HERE

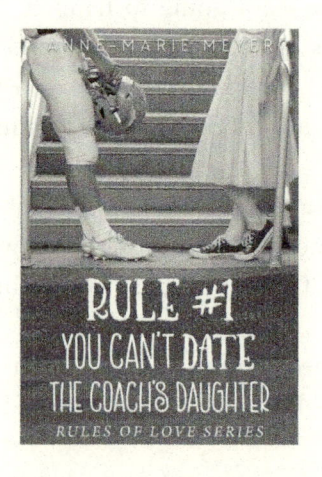

Want MORE Christmas Romance?
Grab Anne-Marie's next YA Romance
My Christmas Break Mistake
HERE

JOIN THE NEWSLETTER

Want to learn about all of Anne-Marie Meyer's new releases plus amazing deals from other authors?
Sign up for her newsletter today and get deals and giveaways!
PLUS a free novella, Love Under Contract

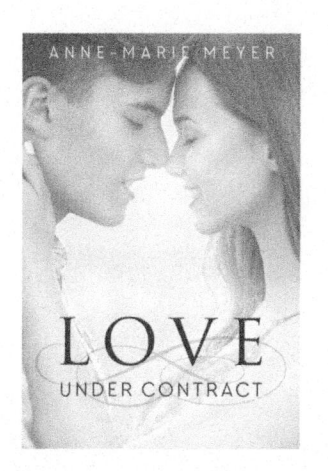

TAKE ME TO MY FREE NOVELLA!

OTHER BOOKS BY ANNE-MARIE MEYER

Clean Adult Romances

Forgetting the Billionaire

Book 1 of the Clean Billionaire Romance series

Forgiving the Billionaire

Book 2 of the Clean Billionaire Romance series

Finding Love with the Billionaire

Book 3 of the Clean Billionaire Romance series

Falling for the Billionaire

Book 4 of the Clean Billionaire Romance series

Fixing the Billionaire

Book 5 of the Clean Billionaire Romance series

The Complete Billionaire Series

The Whole Series for $9.99

Marrying a Cowboy

Book 1 of a Fake Marriage series

Fighting Love for the Cowboy

Book 1 of A Moose Falls Romance

Marrying an Athlete

Book 2 of a Fake Marriage series

Marrying a Billionaire

Book 3 of a Fake Marriage series

Marrying a Prince

Book 4 of a Fake Marriage series

Marrying a Spy

Book 5 of a Fake Marriage series

Second Chance Mistletoe Kisses

Book 1 of Love Tries Again series

CLEAN YA ROMANCES

Rule #1: You Can't Date the Coach's Daughter

Book 1 of the Rules of Love series

Rule #2: You Can't Crush on Your Sworn Enemy

Book 2 of the Rules of Love series

Rule #3: You Can't Kiss Your Best Friend

Book 3 of the Rules of Love series

Rule #4: You Can't Misinterpret a Mistletoe Kiss

Book 4 of the Rules of Love series

ABOUT THE AUTHOR

Anne-Marie Meyer lives in MN with her husband, four boys, and baby girl. She loves romantic movies and believes that there is a FRIENDS quote for just about every aspect of life.

Connect with Anne-Marie on these platforms!
anne-mariemeyer.com

Made in the USA
Monee, IL
17 September 2020